Lesbian Lust With My Professor: The Series

After Classes

After Hours

Aftermath

Aftertaste

Kitty Keen

Copyright © 2024 by Kitty Keen

This book is for ADULT AUDIENCES ONLY. It contains substantial sexually explicit scenes with graphic language which may be considered offensive by some readers.

All sexually active characters in this work are 18 years of age or older.

All rights reserved.

No part of this publication may be reproduced, distributed, or transmitted in any form or by any means, including photocopying, recording, or other electronic or mechanical methods, without the prior written permission of the publisher, except as permitted by U.S. copyright law. For permission requests, contact [include publisher/author contact info].

The story, all names, characters, and incidents portrayed in this production are fictitious. No identification with actual persons (living or deceased), places, buildings, and products is intended or should be inferred.

Book Cover by Steph Brothers

Contents

Contents

After Classes

Book 1

Chapter 1

I TUG ON THE door of my half-dead hatchback, finally resorting to giving it a swift kick, which is a dumb-ass move in these slouchy knit boots. At least the door comes open, with a loud creaking sound to accompany the light swearing that's spilling from my mouth.

I slide into the driver's seat, pull out my cell and check for messages.

One from my mom, one from my kid sister Jeanette, and another from mom. With a shake of my head, I dump the phone in the shotgun seat.

"You two need to learn to communicate with each *other*," I mutter. "I have too much going on to be your damn go-between."

I turn the key in the ignition and the tiny engine whimpers awake with a sputtering cough.

"Come on, you bitch. Don't die on me now." Some other day, maybe it wouldn't bother me so much to miss classes. College is boring, and sitting still is the hardest thing in the world.

But this is one of my two weekly classes with Professor Charlton. Tall, sleek, sexy and oh-so-composed. At all times.

Half the time I want to be her. The other half...well, I've always thought of myself as straight, but that woman has me sitting on the fence. And fantasizing about sitting on...well, other things.

I pinch my wrist, a habit I developed in my early teens. It started out as nothing. It was a placeholder, of sorts. I did it as a reminder. Whenever I realized my thoughts were veering off track, I found a quick burst of sharp pain could bring me back on task.

Of course, it only ever works when I realize I've gone off on some tangent. There's never any guarantee I will.

That little behavior also scores me plenty of withering looks; from teachers, students, counselors, and my mom. I'm not an idiot, and I know exactly what people see when they look at me.

Book smart but emotionally stunted is a pairing I hear a lot. *No impulse control.* That's the one that really burns at me.

If only they knew. For every smart-ass, TMI comment I blurt out loud, there are dozens I somehow keep inside. And I achieve that miracle with nothing more than a quick little pinch of my wrist. What's that if not impulse control?

But I'm pretty sure everyone sees my pinching as a gateway drug. Something that'll lead to cutting and tattoos and drugs laced with pesticides. Mom sure seems to think that, at least.

I've proven them all wrong on that score. So far. Though I'm totally down for some ink, if I can ever get the money together.

My crappy engine clears its throat, but at least it keeps running, so I pull away from the curb. I head for the main road, accidentally conducting a performance of *concerto for car horns* as I blind-merge into a gap between a semi and an SUV.

I wave a half-assed apology and hope that's enough. The guy in the Chevy behind me looks royally pissed, but if push comes to shove I can usually pout my way out of trouble. And if my lips fail me, there's always my tits.

In this tight crop top, with my stupidly tiny cutoff shorts, I should be able to swing things my way. It's hardly lecture-hall-appropriate clothing, but who ever said Giselle Belmont was appropriate?

A moment later, I change lanes, earning a fresh blast of horns. Where the hell did that Corolla come from anyway?

And did I just get a text? It's hard to tell with all those damn car horns.

I scrabble around on the floor for my cellphone and check again for messages, narrowly avoiding a guy who's stepped out into the crosswalk.

Did I just run a red light? Nah, it's probably fine. People always walk against the signal, anyway.

I make absolutely certain to stop at the next light, and my mind idles along with the car. Thinking about my mom, and how she always chose my kid sister over me. And how that's blown up in her face now Jeanette's had enough of being over-parented.

Thinking about how I came to college a hundred miles from home just to get some space from their bickering, only to now have that bickering sent to me in pixel form.

Thoughts of college inevitably bring me back to Professor Charlton, and that clears my mind of all other information.

What is it about her that has me so fascinated? Curious, in more ways than one.

I mean, maybe I'm just crushing on her because she's the most powerful person in my life right now. Maybe it'll pass as soon as the right guy comes along and claims my cherry.

Nobody knows much about the prof's private life, either, so the mystery that surrounds her is another delicious hook that has me dangling.

Everyone can see she has a bod built for sin, even though she hides it. Dark skirt suits, thick-rimmed glasses, immaculate makeup. She nearly always wears her long hair in the tightest of buns. Once in a while—I guess when she feels whimsical—she rocks a ponytail, but it's still tight as fuck.

But then she sends those damned mixed messages, wearing sheer black stockings and crazy high stilettos. The kind of shoes I'd break my whole legs in, not just my ankles.

And all of that only makes her even more fascinating to my squirrel brain. This, despite the fact she's so annoyingly exact, all the time. Pedantic, really. She's the anti-me.

Oh, but then there's her accent. Upper-class English. Like, British English. All snooty and well-mannered, and severe as hell when anyone talks out of turn.

Her style of lecturing utterly commands attention, and seriously, who am I to ignore her? With that crisp, cool accent, and a flowing alto voice that I could listen to all day and night. I think her voice could soothe me to sleep just as easily as it turns me the hell on.

The horn from the car behind me cuts through my thoughts to let me know the light's gone green.

I manage to take off without stalling, and give the driver behind me a quarter-wave. The kind where you only use one of your four available fingers.

For the millionth time, I try to understand my weakness when it comes to Professor Alicia Charlton. Of course, there's my suspect relationship with my mom, but can I really be that much of a walking cliché?

There has to be more to it than that, surely. Whatever it is, all I know is that when Prof Charlton's in charge, I'm all ears. Well, three-quarters ears, one-quarter clit.

And I know it's not just that she's so damn beautiful. And tall and sleek and just...in control of the universe, or something. It's the little quirks she has that have me fascinated with her.

It's the clipped tone of her words, and their precise delivery. The way she touches her glasses, and narrows her eyes, every time she has to utter a dirty word. It doesn't seem to matter that it's part of the course. It really seems to bug her.

That only makes her even more fascinating to me. Our subject matter of late has been addiction, sex, and all manner of nasty and delicious vices, and it seems with each new taboo, the professor closes herself away just a little more.

A lecturer on sexuality who gets coy. What tasty secrets might she be hiding? Was her daddy some kind of ruthless disciplinarian? Did she get bullied at her fancy private school in the countryside? Spanked by the nuns in Catholic school?

Does she have a mistress? Does she *want* one?

Oh, what the hell? I swear I'm straight. I mean, mostly, at least. And for all I know, so is Professor Charlton.

But let's face facts: she could get it. If she told me to, I'd drop to my knees for that woman. What happens from there, I'm not sure. All I know is that I need her approval as much as I need my next meal.

I know the dirty little fantasies I'm playing in my head could never happen in reality anyway, of course. It's totally against policy for a lecturer to even take a student to dinner as a platonic friendship kinda thing. Anything more...*intimate* than that is way off the table.

Pinch.

Holy hell, that one hurt. But I had to do it, to stop myself zoning out behind the wheel some more. And it's all Professor Charlton's fault, for making me think about her. Especially in *that* way, since I'm definitely not even into women. Probably.

The thick traffic has me feeling claustrophobic. Not to mention as antsy as hell. I need to get to campus pronto, and into the lecture hall. That way I can drink in as much time with the Prof as possible.

Chapter 2

I TAKE MY SEAT in the third row and wriggle in place until my ass finds an agreeable spot. I open my laptop and lean against the hard backrest of the lecture hall seat.

It's the kind of chair they'd give you in hell, but that level of discomfort actually works in my favor. I can use it like an ersatz wrist-pinch, to draw my focus back in if it ever wanders. And holy hell, when Professor Charlton speaks, my mind wanders like sparks from a brush fire.

By letting the hard backrest poke into me like that, it also means I can have both hands free to type at all times. I just need to make sure I'm taking notes about the lecture, and not writing fan fiction about the prof's delicious bod. I'm no author, but some of my little daydreams have been pretty fucking hot to read back.

As the other students file in I have my eyes pointed to the laptop screen, but my attention is much more focused on the door to Professor Charlton's office.

Even though it's closed, she must have a window open inside. Every time the breeze blows, it rattles the door and makes my heart jump. Because every time, it makes me sure she's about to step out. That the woman who stars in every one of my silly, outlandish fantasies is about to walk into the hall and complete me.

Jesus, I'm a fucking basket case when it comes to that woman.

It's almost as if Professor Charlton can read my thoughts, the way she walks into the lecture hall right at this moment. I even fancy I can hear heavenly trumpets sounding, announcing her entrance.

"All right. Please take your seats, ragamuffins."

I bite into my lip to stop myself smiling at the term *raga-muffins*. I've heard her use it on everyone from high school students to university staff...even a campus security guard one time. For Professor Charlton, pretty much anyone under the age of 25 qualifies to be called *ragamuffin*.

Even though I know the prof's first name, I can't imagine ever using it. Never out loud, and maybe not even inside my head.

If the prof ever said *call me Alicia* I think my heart just might stop. And my pussy would totally melt.

The thought of that—of Professor Charlton treating me in such an intimate way—has me pinching my wrist like I'm plucking a Thanksgiving turkey.

If I keep that up I'll form a callous before too long, but the woman just drives me wild. From the pounding of my heart, to the pulsing between my legs, Professor Charlton is pretty much my queen.

The pinching is the only way I can deal with it. I limit myself to doing it on my wrist while I'm in public. But in private, I move down to where it does the most good.

Right on my clit.

I wriggle in my seat again, getting myself as close to comfortable as possible, ready for the crisp, fluent tones of my fantasy woman to start.

I gaze through my lowered eyelashes at the lush bow of Professor Charlton's mouth, holding my breath in anticipation.

"Today, we shall be looking at the effect pain can have in eliciting obedience." God, it's like she's tailor-made this lecture for me. My fingers tremble over the laptop keys as the prof continues. "Furthermore, we shall move on to examine the subsequent use of that obedience in the seeking of worldly pleasures."

The clear, musical timbre of her voice, as it warmly caresses those potent syllables, has me curling my toes inside my stupid boots. I close my eyes and swim in the sound for a moment.

As the heat between my legs grows more intense than ever, I begin to imagine a slightly different scene. One where Professor Charlton is seated behind me. Where my fantasy lover leans forward and murmurs to me.

Only she's not making small talk. She's uttering soft, filthy words to me. The kinds of words that make her pause when she says them. Her warm, sweet breath buffeting my hair, and drifting down the side of my neck.

I picture reaching my hand back, to caress Professor Charlton's smooth, luscious face, my palm meeting her cheek, silk against silk.

In my fantasy, the Prof leans into my touch before she draws my fingers into the smooth heat of her mouth. And she suckles on them, makes them as wet as a river. Gets them ready so I can plunge them into the burning depths of her sopping wet cunt while she directs my every move.

Ohh...fuck.

I squeeze the skin of my wrist between my fingers and twist it like I'm starting my car. The pain bites into my consciousness and races up the length of my arm. That's a delicious hard thrill all on its own, even without the resonant tones of Professor Charlton resounding in my ears.

It's such a thrill that I do it again, even harder. So hard, in fact, that I cry out in blissful agony.

Professor Charlton's cool voice cuts through the moment. "What is the kerfuffle up there?"

I jump in place like the chair's electrocuted. I really need to find my focus. Even the pinching isn't working for me today.

I summon the courage to glance down at Professor Charlton, but find an expression on her face that's far closer to anger than calm.

It takes me a moment to swallow the ball of tension in my throat, and I lower my eyes. Disappointing my fantasy woman is the last thing I want to do. "I'm sorry, Professor Charlton."

Thankfully, she lets the matter drop and resumes the lecture. I breathe out and try to recapture the essence of my little fantasy trip.

It's no good. My concentration is totally blown—as usual. Heat still simmers between my thighs but Professor Charlton's disappointment has sure turned off the burner.

I ride out the rest of the lecture filled with tension and need. The hot, tingling ache inside my pussy will definitely need my attention, sooner rather than later. No way I can drive safely under the influence of lust.

I guess I'll have to rub one out in the bathroom straight after the lecture. At the very least I'll probably need to wring my panties out.

Pinch.

"All right, ragamuffins. I will see you all on Thursday."

As the rest of the students stand and pack, leaving as quickly as they can, I sit in place. I have two days until I'll see Professor Charlton again. Or is it three? Fuck, what day is it, even?

In the end, it barely matters. This is my last chance to soak myself in her presence on this current day. I have to milk it for all it's worth. Not to mention if I try to stand up in the Professor's presence, I'll stumble like a newborn foal. The woman has my legs all gelatinous with need.

I watch her perfect, long-fingered hands as she plays them across the surface of the desk.

Pinch.

I can't stop wishing she'd put those hands on my body instead.

Pinchpinch.

Finally, when I can find no way to delay any longer, I tentatively stand. I've barely taken three steps when Professor Charlton speaks directly to me.

"I will see you before you leave."

Chapter 3

Oh, god. I'm so busted. Like, I haven't even done any-thing wrong, but my belly is filled with cold stones, any-way.

I stare down at the Professor, panic filling my veins with ice and fire. Both at once. "M–me?"

"Yes you, Miss Belmont. There is no-one else."

Then she turns and walks back into her office.

For a moment my knees tremble, threatening to make good on their earlier promise to turn all new-born with lust.

Just to hear Professor Charlton say my name has pretty much stopped my breath. But the fact she actually knows it at all sends sparks of desire exploding through me.

I already know she's intense and precise in everything she says, but there was a tone in her voice I don't recall hearing before. So when I ruminate over all the possible meanings of her words—there is no-one else—it gives my heart a fresh jolt.

I shove my still-open laptop under my arm and hook my bag over my other elbow, stumbling slightly on the stairs as I hurry down to Professor Perfect.

"What did you need, uh, ma'am?" *Fuck.*

"Ma'am? Did you recently enlist in the armed forces, Miss Belmont?"

I swallow heavily and take a breath. "No, ma'am. I mean, Professor Charlton."

The Professor lowers her tall, luscious body into the chair behind her leather-topped desk, every movement steady and sedate, as though she choreographed them the moment she woke this morning.

"Miss Belmont. It hasn't escaped my notice that our current subject matter appears to cause you some level of discomfort."

She's right, but I doubt she understands exactly what the cause of that discomfort is.

God, I've never been this close to her for such a prolonged period. Okay, it's only like a minute and a half so far, but it still has my heart pounding and my pussy mewing.

Pinch.

My little trick brings my mind back to the here and now, where Professor Charlton is still speaking.

The sexy older woman pushes her glasses up her nose with a finger. Her nails are all as elegant as she is. Long and glistening with perfect French tips. Nails that could leave delicious red scratches down my back. That could dig into my nipples like teeth.

Fuck.

The Prof raises an eyebrow, as if she can read my mind. It wouldn't be hard. I'm sure my dirty thoughts must be writing themselves all over my face. Why else would my cheeks be so fucking hot?

But the professor says nothing about it. Just continues with what she was saying before.

"Now, I am aware this is none of my business, and let me be clear that I'm not seeking confirmation here..."

"Um...y–yes?"

"If you are as...*inexperienced* as I believe you to be, then perhaps my course would be a better fit for you in another year or two."

My entire face glows hot with embarrassment. It seeps down my throat and I can feel it painting my chest as well. The prof can tell that I'm...that I'm a virgin? That I don't know what the hell I'm doing in her classes?

"In addition, you appear to lack a certain level of discretion. I base this assessment on your behavior during my lectures."

Oh shit. Oh, fuck. I can't let her cut me. I swear it will feel like a *literal* cut if she removes me from her life.

I mean, from her *course*, of course.

"Please, Professor Charlton? I can fix...I mean, I'll..." I'll what? Go and get laid before Thursday? I mean, I guess I could. This is college, after all. I just have no interest in college boys. Or maybe in boys at all.

The prof catches my full attention by leaning her elbows on the desk and making a platform with her threaded hands, to rest her beautiful chin on. It's a nothing kind of move. The kind of nothing move that has me biting my lip. She's just so controlled.

"Please calm yourself, Miss Belmont."

Once again, hearing my name in her voice sends a delicious quiver up and down my spine. Without thinking about it, I snare my wrist between my thumb and finger, and I twist the skin like hell.

The pain brings me back to earth, and I'm able to focus again. I even manage a shaky smile.

Professor Charlton stands up and comes around the desk, her stilettos clicking on the hard floor. She's already tall, and those heels just have her towering over me. If I look straight ahead, all I'll see is the soft depth of her cleavage, so I do everything in my power to maintain eye contact instead.

Jesus, she smells so fucking good. Like some kind of orchid, with a fruity undertone. Good enough to eat.

She stops a few inches from me and looks down on me. I've never felt so small in my life. She reaches out and brushes my hair back over my ears.

"Why on earth do you do that, Miss Belmont?"

"D–do what?"

I'm still lost in her eyes, even behind her glasses, so I don't notice her moving. The next thing I feel is her surprisingly warm hand as she curls her fingers around my wrist. She raises my hand until it's between us, then turns it so the soft underside is toward me.

"This," she murmurs, and then strokes her thumb over the reddened skin where I've been torturing myself. Her touch is so soft, but my skin is so raw. And my squirrely little brain mixes up the messages. Tells me that professor sexy here is the one who inflicted the pain.

Far from making me flinch, though, it just makes me want her that much more. I'm starting to think I'll do anything at all to please this woman. And that I'll let her do anything she pleases to me. Give me pleasure, inflict pain, or even better, some heady cocktail of the two.

She leans closer, and her breath courses across my cheek. It's warm and sweet, and it caresses my skin like ghostly fingers.

"You really are quite the conundrum, Miss Belmont," she says, her voice so low it's like a thought more than a sound.

"I'm sorry."

The prof narrows her eyes immediately, though I don't get the sense she's angry at me. I swear it's more like she's angry for me.

"Giselle," she says, and holy fucking fuck. I'm already lost in her cultured English accent. To have her say my given name is a pleasure that defies reason.

But to have her pronounce it in that liquid and lyrical way that French people do...I'm just about a puddle on the floor.

"Yes?" My own voice is a tiny squeak.

"Giselle, would you please close the door?"

I've turned on the spot and have a hold of the handle before common sense kicks in. "Wait...is that...is that even allowed?" Students and faculty aren't meant to be alone together, after all.

"No, Giselle. Of course it isn't."

"Oh."

I pause while I try to understand exactly what she wants. What I'm supposed to do. Professor Charlton sits on the front edge of her desk and regards me with cool interest.

When she removes her glasses and tilts her head ever so slightly, I realize that she's leaving the decision up to me. To break the rules or follow them. And then I know for certain—rules be damned—I'm going to do whatever this woman tells me.

Starting with closing the door. Just for good measure, I lock it before stumbling back toward the prof. Christ, she's the picture of composure and I'm just a wild mess in trailer trash clothing and unworkable shoes.

"What is it you require, Giselle?"

I have no idea what she's talking about, and I'm sure she can tell. I've never been so confused in all my life. Or so fucking aroused.

Professor Charlton takes my hand and pulls me a little closer, and she strokes my wrist again with her thumb. It's still sore, but the pain is somehow comforting. I even let out a tiny sigh at her touch.

"You need help to manage your urges. Don't you, cherie?"

The breath I draw sounds like it's made from steam. "W–what did you call me?"

She squeezes my wrist a little tighter, awakening a taste of the residual ache from my pinching. Then she presses the palm of her other hand to my cheek. "Cherie." Again, she says it with the richness of a native French speaker, where the r sound actually hovers somewhere between a w and a y, and I fall a little harder for this woman. Still, I feel I should be up front with her.

"Ma'am...um, Professor Charlton, I should proba-bly...I—I'm not a lesbian."

She leans closer, and her lips are so soft and plump, and she's so damn perfect. When her beautiful mouth is almost touching my ear, she speaks in a low murmur. "What a coincidence. Neither am I, cherie."

Then she presses those luscious lips to my cheek, and I put my hand over the back of hers as I lean into the touch. The moan I let out sounds like I'm singing, and it only stops when Professor Charlton takes my mouth in hers.

Chapter 4

It's not just the first time I've ever kissed another woman. It's the first time I've ever been kissed at all, and the sensation is so intense it makes me dizzy. She tastes of honey and mint, and it's all I can do to keep myself together.

She threads her fingers up into my hair and I go all limp in her arms. This is so, so wrong. It's perfect. We can't do this. I can't stop.

And then, it's Professor Charlton who stops. She breaks our kiss, and traces my wet lips with her thumb. "My goodness, cherie," she whispers, the warmth of her breath delightful but a poor substitute for the heat of her mouth.

"What are you doing to me?" I whisper, and I'm certain there's fear all over my face.

"You have so much to learn, cherie."

"Uh, f–for your course?"

"About life. And yourself. All of which will benefit you in my classes." She takes hold of my shoulders and spins me on the spot until I have my back pressed against her. "And who better than I to teach you?"

"Oh..."

Professor Charlton skims her luscious lips across the shell of my ear, her breath gushing in like the tide for a moment. She takes hold of my hips as she kisses the side of my neck, and I whimper like a puppy.

"Oh, cherie," she says, more of a moan than a word. "You are quite the temptation."

She slides her hands up my body until she has my breasts cupped in her palms. I arch my back as if I'm presenting them to her, and she sinks her teeth into the curve where my neck meets my shoulder.

"Oh, my god..."

I don't know what to do with my hands. I flutter them in mid-air like drunken doves until Professor Charlton takes hold of one and guides that arm behind my back. She repeats it with the other and then holds both my wrists together, locked in her hand, as she peppers my neck and cheek with soft kisses. I'm not exactly powerless to resist her, here. I'm just unwilling to.

"Ohhh, professor..."

I can feel her smile against my neck as she gently bites me again. She squeezes my wrists tighter as she pinches my nipple between her thumb and finger.

It's like a bolt of lightning has shot from my breast to my clit. I'm throbbing, aching with need.

"P–Professor..."

"As your professor, I must officially reprimand you for your attire."

Dammit. I mean, I knew it was inappropriate, but I kinda hoped—

"But unofficially, I find your raw beauty to be intensely eye-catching, cherie. Especially presented as it is, here and now."

The prof rolls her hand, twisting my breast slightly, before trailing her fingers down my bare belly. She pauses at the top of my shorts for a moment, as though making a decision. Or waiting for me to protest—which I know I should do, but I also know I won't.

Then she works the button open, and I let out a long, breathy moan. When she draws my zipper down, everything suddenly feels intensely real. Like I've just woken from a dream. I whip my head around to whisper my fears to her.

"Professor Charlton, what if someone—"

"Shh," she says, and presses her lips to mine once more. She draws my tongue into her mouth and bites down on it, and I swear it works even better than a pinch on my wrist. It's a sweet little sharpness that has me sucking in a gasp that draws the air from her body, not from the room around us.

Professor Charlton slips her fingers inside my panties, and down over my hair free mound. She drives them in against my slicked up slit and makes a low growling sound, like a hunting lioness. Or I guess it's more like a cougar.

"Cherie," she moans again as she hooks her fingers. I'm so, so fucking wet that she just glides straight up inside me. I've never had anything in there except my own fingers, but even those have never felt as fucking good as this.

"Ohhh, Jesus," I whisper, and my knees buckle as she grinds her fingers against my clit. I throw one hand up around the back of Professor Charlton's neck, just to keep from collapsing to the floor. My tall, powerful fantasy woman is my only support, and she's all I need.

She nuzzles her mouth against my ear and whispers to me. "I fancy you must be an utter treat for the senses down here, my little pudding."

God. If anyone else, at any time, had called me their *little pudding*, I would have laughed in their faces and then probably tossed a drink on them. Even if I had to go to a bar and buy one first.

Hearing that silly little name in Professor Charlton's cultured voice, with her long, elegant fingers pleasuring me at the same time, has me teetering right on the edge of climax.

She's the one who throws me over that precipice, though, as she bites my neck, and I come so hard I almost lose consciousness. I'm floating in space, and my skin is getting peppered by the sand-sized remnants of some world I once knew that's just been blown to pieces.

Professor Charlton keeps me from escaping her orbit by holding me rigidly against her lush body; one hand in my panties, one on my breast, her mouth attached to my neck and pulsing along with the last traces of my orgasm.

I can barely keep my legs from collapsing, and the racing of my breath sounds like a timber yard. And yet behind me, the professor stands tall and calm. Not a hair out of place. Not a bead of sweat on her skin. Even her breathing is soft and gentle.

It's as if she hasn't been affected at all by what we've just done, whereas I look and feel as if I've been hit by a tsunami.

And then Professor Charlton slides her fingers out of me, slips her hand free from my panties, and holds it up in front of us. My arousal glistens on her skin, and my scent seems to fill the air.

"Marvelous." For the first time, my professor sounds like she's been moved in some way. She glides her hand through the air in smooth arcs, like she's a queen waving to the unwashed masses, and stronger bursts of my fragrance waft across to greet us.

I can't take my eyes away from her perfectly manicured fingers, even as she glides them past my face. A moment later there's a soft smacking noise, and when I turn to look, Professor Charlton is suckling on those fingers. She draws in a long breath through her nose, and then licks one finger like it's a slender cock. As if she plans to drink every trace of me from her own skin.

"Mm. Delightful." It's at once the warmest and coolest she's ever sounded. "Have you ever tasted yourself, my little pudding?"

"N–no." I jill off like crazy, every damn day. Especially since this woman entered my life. But I've never been brave enough to put those fingers in my mouth afterward.

She holds her hand toward me, palm down, like a noblewoman waiting for a servant to help her out of her carriage. When I hesitate, she guides her fingers to my lips

and strokes the bottom one, leaving traces of me there. I flick my tongue out, just to appease her, but the moment I get the first taste of my juices, I pause.

"Ohhh..."

Professor Charlton presses her cheek against mine, and hooks her fingers. "Would my little pudding like some more?"

"P–Please?"

She glides her fingers inside my mouth, turning her face so she can sink her teeth into my cheek, just lightly. "You are the most delicious little treat, cherie." As I suckle on her fragrant fingers, she slides her lips across my skin and takes my earlobe between her perfect teeth.

Oh, fuck, I'm getting all wet again, and my pussy is throbbing so hard I'm sure it's going to explode. I can't speak with my mouth full like it is, so I just whimper.

Professor Charlton eases her fingers free of my mouth but leaves them pressed to my lips. Then she comes around to kiss me again and we fence with our tongues around the barrier of her fingers. I taste myself as much as I taste her, and just the thought of that—of truly tasting her—has me on the verge of coming again. What better way to please my professor than to put my mouth between her legs?

And then it all stops. Professor Charlton breaks our kiss and pushes me away from her. I lose all the strength and stability I had when I leaned on her, and it takes every bit of my will power just to keep from falling to my knees.

Chapter 5

"W—what?"

I turn to face her, wondering what I've done wrong. She's still the picture of cool serenity. Not a hair out of place. Not a button undone. Not even a crease in her damn skirt.

"Professor Charlton? Don't you want me to...um...?" I point vaguely at her body with both hands rather than risk tossing the words out into the real world.

"This has been an excellent start, Giselle. I take great encouragement from your willingness and...your adaptability."

Start? "I'm not following."

The professor comes over to me, and for a moment she's my entire universe again. She plants a tiny, playful kiss on the tip of my nose, and my head whirls with confusion. This woman is the fucking queen of mixed messages.

"Sweet cherie," she hums. "It's vital to me that you not be overwhelmed. Patience is not merely a skill. It's a tool and even a pleasure all of its own."

"I, uh..."

She curls her beautiful mouth into a tiny half-smile, and then shocks me by gliding to her knees. She takes a soft hold of my hips and plants a lingering kiss on my belly, just above my navel. Slowly, sweetly, she glides lower, flicking my skin with her hot pink tongue. I know my eyes must be like two bright full moons as I gaze down at her. Wondering if this is going where I think—where maybe I hope—it's going.

When she reaches the top of my panties, Professor Charlton takes a hold of them in her teeth and pulls them away from my skin. Just a tiny way, and then she lets them slap back against me. "Mm. Such a delectable treat you are, my little pudding. But I can hardly lecture you on the virtues of patience and then immediately...dive headfirst into the temptation before me."

Oh, god. Dive. Dive right in.

The prof takes hold of my shorts and refastens the button. She peppers me with kisses from hip to hip and every spot in between as she fumbles for my zipper. When my shorts are all done up again, Professor Charlton strokes her hands down the outsides of my thighs, and then stands. How is it possible she makes me feel entirely wanted and completely rejected all in the one move?

"Please, Miss Belmont," she says, and it cuts me like paper. An hour ago, just hearing Professor Charlton use my surname like that had me yearning for more. Now, all it does is put a wall between us. Can't I be her little pudding, still? "Do not misunderstand me."

"But I don't understand anything, professor. Like, ever."

Her expression wavers just slightly away from cool and steely. Her mouth softens a little but it's her eyes that change the most. Deep brown that somehow grows deeper. "I fancy I would gain great perspective if I were to meet her. Or him. But I strongly suspect it's a woman."

"Professor?"

"Whoever it is who's told you that you're worthless, cherie. They've told you so often that you truly believe them."

I wince as if she's slapped me, and for sure I'm only seconds away from tears. "I have to..." I can't even speak anymore, so I scoop up my shit and fumble with it all the way to the door of Professor Charlton's office.

It takes me a whole lot of juggling of bag and laptop so I can unlock the door. Before I open it, she's behind me, both her hands pressed to the dark wood, keeping it closed.

"Giselle," she says, so quietly I feel it more than I hear it.

I take a long breath in, then let it out slowly. "What?"

"Wait just a moment, cherie."

I rest my forehead against her door and listen as she walks back to her desk, her stilettos clicking on the wooden floor as she goes. The soft sound of a drawer opening and clos-ing and then she clickety-clicks her way back to me.

"Take this, please." She slips a charcoal grey business card into the pocket of my shorts. "I will see you tonight. 8pm. Sharp."

"But..."

"Or I will not."

My body tightens at her words, without me even realizing I've done so.

"I repeat, cherie; do not misunderstand me. This will have no bearing on your grade. You have every right to refuse."

I slip the card out of my pocket and read it. All it has is a street address, embossed into the otherwise flat card. No phone number, no other identification. How often does she do this, that she has a printed card for it?

"Tonight," Professor Charlton repeats, and I already know I'm going to be there. "Eight o'clock. Will that tatty old automobile of yours make the journey?"

Woah, just how much does she already know about me? I stand there, fondling the tiny embossed bumps on the card, and I nod, even though I can't honestly be sure my car will even start.

Then again, for an opportunity like this, I'll catch the bus. Or steal a friggin' skateboard from the neighbor's kid. I turn to leave, but her voice freezes me to the spot for a moment.

"I very much look forward to your sparkling company tonight, Giselle."

The sound of my name in her beautiful mouth works wonders on my body all over again. Without another thought, I pinch my wrist almost hard enough to draw blood, hoping that with my back turned, Professor Charlton won't notice. No such luck.

"Tonight, my little pudding, you shall discover a far more constructive and creative way to channel that river of frustration."

"Yes, Profess—uh, yes ma'am." I don't know why, but I just have an inkling that's the name I'll be calling this woman tonight.

As I step through the door and into the lecture hall, she stops me again. "Miss Belmont? As alluring as your scant attire might be, I expect a more...formal wardrobe tonight."

A little burst of panic fills my belly. Formal? The closest thing I have to formal wear is my black yoga pants, and a man's checked shirt I got from the local goodwill. What the hell am I going to do?

"Giselle?"

I swallow the rhinoceros of tension in my throat, and say the only words I can think of.

"Yes, ma'am."

END OF BOOK 1

After Hours

Book 2

Chapter 1

My legs betray me all the way back to my shitty little car. I drop my bag twice on the walk, but thank fuck I keep a tight hold on my laptop. No way can I afford to replace it. I can barely make rent as it is, and now I have some clothes shopping to do.

My pallid bank account scares me more in this moment than it usually does. Mostly because I really want to make a splash with the prof tonight. I mean, she didn't say I had to dress *formally*, but she did say *more formal*. I could probably wrap myself in a blanket and it'd be more formal than what I'm wearing right now.

I flop into the driver's seat and close the door, letting out a long sigh. For the first time since I moved out of home I kinda wish I was closer to the place. At least closer to

Jeanette, since she's about my size, and her wardrobe has always been much fancier than mine. Thanks again, mom.

I can't put all the blame on her, though. Some of it should go to Jeanette, because she's never been afraid to just ask for shit. I've always felt like I should wait until shit got offered.

So, yeah. A fuck ton of the blame for my situation has to go to me. Naturally. I've consistently failed to save any money for a rainy day. This doesn't qualify exactly as a rainy day but holy fuck, I'm so wet anyway.

I try to pin down exactly what I'm feeling, and the truth is, I'm not sure. I'm feeling a million things all at once, from every direction. But all those things zero in on one truth. The way Professor Charlton treats me.

It's not one thing. It's a whole range of them. How she touched me so intimately. How she made me come so hard. That she spoke to me almost maternally.

Her words of praise and even support swirl around my head like a tornado, and they never seem to settle in a coherent pattern. They just twist and twirl and make me crazy. It takes me a moment before I realize I have the skin of my wrist trapped between finger and thumb once more.

One thing I know for sure, I'm desperate for the prof to touch me again. Even more than that. I'm beyond desperate to touch her. That's why I can't afford to miss this...whatever it is, tonight. Dinner? Games night? Netflix and chill?

Christ, I'm wet. And so fucking needy. I slide my hand into my panties and glide my fingers over my hot and swollen pussy.

Fuck, I'm not just wet, I'm drenched, even though it's not even a quarter hour since Professor Charlton made me come like a fountain.

I pause with my fingers in place, replaying everything. The soft but solid feel of that woman's body pressed to my back. The pinpoint accuracy of her fingers as she brought me off. The rich blend of fruity and flowery scents from her skin and her perfume.

As I run through the highlights, I make a tight circling motion with my fingers over my clit, and it hits me like a slap with a cold metal spoon. It's such an overwhelming pleasure that it actually hurts. With only a few more grinds of my fingers I'm utterly exploding into another climax.

It's not as good as it was with the prof, though. It's barely even a shadow of that. Just like the taste of me on her fingers was nowhere near enough.

I want more. I need more. I need the taste of *her* on my *lips*.

As I ease my fingers free, I glance up at the parking lot around me. It's only then that I realize how fucking reckless I've been, touching myself like this in public. I don't think I'm in view of the security cameras, but still, anyone could have seen me. Obviously, I'm as flighty as hell, all the time. But I'm not usually so actively careless.

I shove my clean hand into my pocket and take out the card the professor gave me. It seems to thrum with energy, like it's a sex toy. Like it's alive. I run my thumb over the embossed street address, and my breath catches in my throat. For some reason, it's almost like touching my clit again.

I pull up my phone and type the address into the map app. Oh, god, she lives in the middle of the classy suburbs just to the north of campus. What kind of money does this woman come from? Or what has she done in her life up until now to afford that part of town?

Do they even let fucked up old hatchbacks like mine drive on their streets?

It suddenly clicks to me that I don't have time to be messing around here. I need to get home and shower, but before that I absolutely have to figure out what the hell I'm going to wear. And really, my only option is the thrift store. Just have to hope they have something decent, close to my size.

***

My crazy bitch of a car somehow manages to get me all the way to Professor Charlton's house. Or at least, to the address on the card. Maybe she isn't really a professor. Maybe she's a human trafficker, or a controlling owner in a porn studio, and she's planning to get me hooked on drugs so badly I'll do anything for my next hit.

Pinch.

I take a cleansing breath and study the place. It's completely in fitting with the area. Clean lines, manicured lawn, security gates. Otherwise, it's a huge but regular looking modern one-story house. With no lights on anywhere inside as far as I can see.

I flick the cabin light on in my car, punching it two or three times until it finally lights up, and then I check the card again. Yep, this is definitely the place. I'm even a little early, which is totally unlike me.

As I clamber out of the car, I can't help shivering. It's not that cold, but this brand new—to me, at least—dress is pretty sleek and it doesn't leave a whole lot to the imagination. I can't even wear a bra in this thing.

There's also the whole woman walking alone at night factor that's playing on my mind. Sure, I'm in the nice part of town, but that doesn't rule out danger. Bad shit happens to rich people, too. Not often enough, some folks might say.

I wince at my own bitchiness. Growing up poor, smart and flighty has done nothing to prepare me for this moment. And it suddenly feels really goddamn heavy.

I'm here at the understated but beautiful home of a woman I have almost nothing in common with. Not age, not social status, not even intellect. She's so far out of my league she might as well be back home in England.

Pinch.

And then there are the rules. The dammit-all-to-hell, motherfucking rules.

Because let's face it, even if I was here to have tea and fucking crumpets with the prof, that's still out of the question. The school's policy about this is as transparent as my lust for Professor Charlton. We're not just breaking rules. If things go as I hope tonight, we'll be shattering them to pieces.

And yet, I'm not leaving. Sure, my legs quiver with tension in these mid-heels, but that's only because I'm still walking up to the gates. There's a minute until it's 8pm, so I wait. Pinching my wrist for 58 of those fucking seconds.

The moment my cell phone reads 8:00, I press the button on the security gate. Barely three seconds later, there's a buzz, and I push through.

Chapter 2

I BITE INTO MY lip and pinch my wrist. It's a double act now, apparently. The lights in the garden come on as I scamper up the pathway, and the door swings open just as I reach it.

Professor Charlton stands there, in an ankle length dark burgundy dress that's even tighter than her hair buns usually are.

It's both a surprise and a pure delight to see her hair flowing freely. Long, dark caramel tresses that caress her bare shoulders. And of course, her makeup is completely on point.

"Oh my god, you look fucking amazing," I blurt out, then slap my hand over my mouth. Why the hell didn't I just pinch my wrist instead of speaking my silly mind?

"Good evening, Miss Belmont. Do come in."

She makes no move to the side so I have squeeze past her into the hallway. My arm brushes her big boobs as I pass, and that same fruit and floral scent caresses my senses.

The inside of the house reflects the outside. Sparsely-furnished, barely decorated at all. Nothing personal in the front room. Everything neat and crisp and cold. Maybe she's just renting. Or maybe she really does have a dark past and wants to keep it locked away.

"Please, come through," she says, indicating the long hallway with two closed doors either side, and a single open door at the end. All the side doors radiate an air of stiff formality, if that's possible for an inanimate object.

Whatever the truth, I feel certain those doors are all locked. Maybe those are the rooms she keeps her photos and fucking knick-knacks in. Oh, fuck, what if she has a different girl locked up behind each one?

Christ, what the hell is going on with me? The fact the prof invited me here, and I came, is already making a drama of our lives. I don't need to thread more of a dark fantasy through it all.

"You are quite lovely tonight, cherie," Professor Charlton says. "Your attire is a refreshing surprise."

"What, this? Got it from Goodwill. It's a little small for me but it was the closest I could find to—"

Professor Charlton cuts me off, pressing her finger to my lips. "Please, cherie. I give so few compliments. How lovely it would be if you could learn to accept one."

"Sorry."

The prof cocks one eyebrow, and I know she wants to say more. Reprimand me, maybe? Coach me in some way?

Instead, she leads me down to the end of the hallway, and the atmosphere changes instantly. The room is warm and intimate, with warm lighting from a dozen different sources. Downlights, uplights, lanterns.

In the center of the room is a long table with a chair at either end. She pulls out a chair for me and I step into the space it left.

"Have you eaten, cherie?"

"N—never." I turn on the spot and cross my wrists in front of myself. Trying to keep from pinching myself as I blurt out more of my stupid feelings. "I want to, though. With you. So fucking much."

"Really?" Even though I'm gazing at the floor I can tell Professor Charlton has that sexy half-grin on her luscious lips. "You've not eaten food ever before?"

Fuck. I'm so keyed up I'm reading everything wrong.

"Oh. I, um...misunderstood."

Professor Charlton steps forward and puts her hands on my waist. She squeezes my flesh just a little and then pushes me back until my ass hits the end of the table. Then she pats the surface.

Neither of us speaks as I ease myself up until I'm sitting on the tabletop. Professor Charlton brings the chair back in and sits in it. Even then, she's nearly eye level with me.

This tall, sexy woman has me in her thrall. The light touch of her fingers against my ankles makes me jump, and then she eases my heels off my feet.

Then she puts her hands on my bare knees and slides my dress slowly up my thighs. Halfway up she takes a hold of them and pushes my legs wide apart.

"I'm delighted you chose to attend tonight," she says. "I'm afraid the memory of our tryst this afternoon has entirely occupied my mind. I have prepared no dinner."

As she speaks, she strokes her thumbs up and down, caressing the tops of my inner thighs. All of her attention seems to be on my panties. Probably studying the big patch of wetness that's no doubt spreading across them.

"Hmm. In any case, it seems perhaps we should skip straight to dessert. Or as we call it in my country...*pudding*."

Ohhh... "Yes, ma'am."

The professor slides her chair forward, and I find the bravery to meet her halfway. I lean down and she cups my chin as she plants a kiss on me. It's so gentle, it's barely a touch, but it's like a hot streak of lust just pulsed from her lips to my core. I was already wet. Now, I'm fucking soaked.

"Such a delicacy," she murmurs, then tilts my head back so she can kiss the length of my neck. She eases the shoulder straps of my dress down and then gives them a rough yank. My bare tits pop free and I suck in a deep breath of surprise which only makes my girls stand higher and prouder.

Professor Charlton glances from one breast to the other, that same eyebrow slightly raised. I swear she's going to grade my boobs like a term paper.

Then she leans in and takes my nipple into her mouth. She bites it just slightly, and the skin of my neck tingles with want as I writhe my ass against the table.

The prof holds both my shoulder straps in one hand, securing my arms with them. The other hand, she presses to the inside of my thigh. Achingly close to my apex. And as she sucks and teases and bites my nipple, I become a gushing river of desire.

My sexy professor twists the shoulder straps, tightening them until my arms are effectively bound. I've heard about this kind of thing, of course. Even watched a few little porn clips where women get tied up.

It always looked hot, but I never thought it would be *my* kind of thing. Yet here we are, with Professor Charlton binding my arms in a makeshift way, and it's making me crazy with need.

I'm clearly radiating my thoughts and feelings though. The prof makes a sweet little humming sound and lets my nipple slip free of her hot mouth. "My little pudding...it appears you relish restraints. And the freedom they grant."

My mind whirls for a moment. *Restraint* is the last word I'd ever associate with myself. And how can it be a form of freedom if I'm bound in some way?

And yet, I sense a deeper truth in her words. Is this something we can explore? Ohhh...is *that* what those other rooms are for?

Professor Charlton moans with desire as she switches to my other breast, flicking the bud with her lovely long tongue. She releases her grip on my dress and I pull my arms out so I can lean my hands on her shoulders. Otherwise I just might collapse.

My fantasy woman comes up off my breast and takes my mouth in a deep kiss. While she glides her tongue in and out of my mouth, she works my dress down past my hips. She hooks her thumbs into my panties and I lift my ass just long enough that she can strip me bare.

Chapter 3

Oh, god. This is so fucking confronting, and yet it feels perfect. I've never been even partially naked for another person before. Even in her office this afternoon, I still had my shorts and panties on while she fingered me to an incredible climax.

Now I'm sitting on her fancy pants table...without any fancy pants on.

The silliness of my thought blends with the tension I'm already feeling, and it all comes out as a childish little giggle. Professor Charlton swallows that sound and lets out a deep snarl in response that vibrates against my lips like an engine. I don't know if I've displeased her again, or if I'm somehow turning her on even more.

That question is answered a moment later when she stands and presses on my shoulders, guiding me to lie flat on the table. She runs her long, elegant fingers down over my breasts, onto my belly. I have an insane and desperate need to pinch my wrist but it feels as if the table is spinning, and I have to keep my hands flat on it for support.

She leans over me, still fully dressed, and plants a soft kiss on my lips. Then she parts my lips with hers, and she flicks her tongue over mine. It's all so soft and sweet. The gentle kind of kisses I'd give myself if that were possible.

Then she bites my bottom lip, hard enough to make me cry out. It's the most blissful sensation of sweet pain, and it brings me exactly the kind of clarity that my wrist pinches always do.

I can't keep myself from squirming on the table beneath her, and the look on her face tells me she absolutely fucking loves the effect she has on me.

Professor Charlton releases my lip from her teeth and meanders her way down my body, navigating the hills and valleys with gentle touches of her lips.

When the sweet warmth of her breath courses over my bare, wide spread and wet pussy, it's like gravity turns its back on us. I claw my fingers, and I'm scared I'm leaving scratches in her expensive table. I just need to hold on to this planet for a moment longer, and there's no guarantee I can do that if she does what I think she's going to.

"Good gracious," she says, and her words kiss my aching slit like angels wings. Yeah, I'm completely fucking gone. Utterly loopy with need. "You are utterly exquisite, my little pudding."

Her praise is too much. It can't possibly be true, and I sputter out some kind of protest. The prof presses her hand to my belly, stilling me with her actions and calming me with her silence.

Then she leans down and licks me, once, from my asshole all the way up to my clit. I cry out so loudly that it echoes back to me from the corners of the room.

Professor Charlton pauses, her eyes closed and her brow creased with concentration. Then her eyes spring open, wide and clear like she's just taken some kind of upper, and she bites into the soft skin of my inner thigh. It's an even more intense agony than when she bit my lip and it's almost enough to make me come. My legs quiver and I have to grab hold of the table edges just for security.

As she swirls her tongue in slow circles around my clit, I'm lost. I'm gone. I'm flying. I always figured it must be kinda nice to have a mouth on your pussy. There's no way nice would ever be strong enough to describe this sensation.

"Fuck...Professor Charlton..."

She just hums against my tender flesh, and grinds her tongue over every fucking inch of my cunt. From thigh to thigh, from asshole to mound, she soaks me with her perfect mouth and agile tongue.

"Uhhh." I shake my head as my body turns to champagne, the pleasure bubbling up inside me so much and so fast I picture my head popping off and my climax gushing out of me.

Professor Charlton slides her hands up the table until she touches mine. It's like ballet as we thread our fingers together and squeeze, palm to palm, while my sexy professor bites down on my clit.

And then I'm fucking gone. I'm soaring. Utterly exploding.

I'm coming so hard I can barely breathe, and Professor Charlton won't let up. She keeps grinding her tongue over me, flicking her nose against my clit and driving me so wild that I think I might die from the pleasure.

On and on, my body pulses in waves, until finally I'm drained. I'm left panting on her table, my flesh nothing more than a puddle of desire. The prof eases her grip on my hands and I can see I've left little half moon marks in her skin with my nails.

Oh god, is she going to hate me? Was I just too fucking easy? I was, wasn't I? Silly girl. Fuck.

I'm still spread out wide before her, my slick, glistening pussy right there. If anything I'm even more exposed, more vulnerable now than I've ever been.

Instinct takes over and I cross my arms over my body as I try to cover my nakedness. Just as I get a grip on my wrist to pinch it all to hell, Professor Charlton stops me, just by resting her hand on mine.

"Giselle. No shame."

"I don't know what's wrong with me." I shake my head, fighting back the tears. "I'm such a fucking idiot."

I can't slam my legs together while Professor Charlton is between them. So I try to scoot backward away from her.

All I need right now is to hide all these ridiculous feelings. Maybe get into a fetal position and rock myself until I'm calm.

Professor Charlton seems to anticipate my every move, and she grabs me by the hips. She rolls me until I'm on my belly, still sprawled over her table. But now, with my ass pointed to the sexy prof.

"Please," I say. Begging. "I need to..." To work out how to finish that sentence. That's what I need, first. I scrabble at the table and it's like I'm panicked, suddenly.

The sharp impact of Professor Charlton's hand on the cheek of my ass freezes me in place. It's the sound as much as the impact that shocks me. And then, a split second later, the pain utterly ignites in my flesh.

"Fuck!"

She follows up with a slap on the other side, and I swear it's like those old movies. The hysterical woman who inexplicably calms down when someone slaps her cheek. Only I do more than simply calm down.

I fucking melt.

Chapter 4

"VERY GOOD, CHERIE," PROFESSOR Charlton says as she strokes her fingertips softly over the flesh she just tortured. I barely realize what I'm doing as I arch my back, lifting my shoulders so I can turn my head. Before I can lock eyes with the prof, she glides to her knees. Out of sight.

"I see you, Giselle." She leans forward and kisses the hot red skin on one side of my ass. "All the little broken pieces you wish to hide...I see you."

Even though her touch is soft and sweet, like a mother with her baby, I'm instantly calm. And holy fuck, but I'm wet again.

"I *see* you, cherie. And I can help you find your way."

As she speaks, she trails her fingers down the crease between my cheeks, touching everything. All my most sensitive places. I clench, instinctively, and the prof chuckles. "Such a naughty little pudding."

My instinct is to apologize again, but I manage to bite my tongue. Literally. I use it again as a placeholder where I'd normally pinch my wrist.

Professor Charlton glides her hands either side of my right thigh, stroking lightly down both the inside and outside. The hair on the back of my neck bristles in anticipation, and I let out a tiny whimper. When she has hold of my knee, she lifts that leg and pushes it up on top of the table.

I'm standing on only one foot. The rest of me is up on the table, and I swear I must look like a lizard, trying to flee a cat. And in this moment I feel even more exposed to the gorgeous woman behind me than I did before.

"*Magnifique*," Professor Charlton says, and then presses her sexy mouth to my pussy. This time, she's not plunging her tongue in, or grinding my flesh with hers. This is more like a passionate kiss between lovers, as she eases my lips apart with her mouth. Her alto voice grows higher, her moans shorter, as she devours my hot little cunt, over and over.

"Oh, holy fuck," I cry out, as I claw and slap at the table. I'm no longer worried about the marks I might leave. I just have to hang on and hope I don't fall off the edge of the world and into a fiery lake of ecstasy. The prof grips my ass with both hands and squeezes so hard it burns.

I raise my ass, and I pump my hips backward. Professor Charlton's moans turn to snarls of hunger. She turns her head one way and the other, as if desperate to taste every single part of me. When she licks all the way up and tickles my ass hole with her hot, wet tongue, I cry out in pure surprise.

It's so wrong. It's completely forbidden. Oh, god, I can't resist this woman.

As she licks my ass, she rubs my clit, and I feel myself building toward another orgasm. It shouldn't be possible to come so soon after the last one, but there's no stopping it, now.

Professor Charlton slides down and bites my clit, and I'm gone. My body is wracked with perfect tremors and I push up with my arms so I can howl at the moon. Or at least, the ceiling.

When the climax finally ebbs away, I'm barely conscious, floating in a warm, wet bubble of pure pleasure.

Professor Charlton kisses her way up my spine, and she guides me back off the table and into her arms. We stand for a moment, embracing like lovers. Like family. Then she takes her seat again and brings me onto her lap.

It's just instinct that has me curling up into a ball. I lean my head on her plentiful chest, and she strokes my hair.

"Sweet little pudding," she says, her voice low and soothing.

She's still fully clothed. Hasn't even removed her shoes. And here I am, naked as a newborn. Fuck, I'm probably leaving a rich wet patch in the lap of her sleek dress.

"Please, ma'am?" I whisper. "Let me, uh..." How do I even ask to pleasure her?

The prof smiles and kisses my forehead, then guides my legs down until my feet can touch the floor again. We stand together and she leads me back out of the room and into the hallway. She stops outside one of the side doors.

"Please, cherie," she says, and waves her hand toward that door. "If you would care to enter, I will join you momentarily."

She takes a step back as if to give me space to make my own choice. I'm not sure what I want, but I know it involves this gorgeous woman. And whatever is behind door number one.

I take hold of the handle and twist it. The door clicks open, and I step into the darkness. Professor Charlton flicks a switch and a soft, warm glow reveals the room. As I adjust to the low light, I can't help but gasp.

It's a room dedicated to pleasure. There's a four-poster bed, with restraints at each of the corners. There's a broad cabinet along one wall, with a whole lot of leather and metal and things I don't even recognize. And other things I recognize all too clearly.

Sex toys. Well, mostly just dildos and vibrators. So many sizes, shapes and colors.

"Oh...my..."

"Get comfortable, my little pudding." She remains in the hallway and closes the door.

I don't know where to begin. *Comfort* doesn't seem to be the first word that comes to mind, even with a bed that plush and inviting. *Pleasure. Exquisite torture. Sweet, biting pain.* Those are the words that fly into my head, no matter where I look.

With no better ideas, I crawl onto the bed and lie back. O hhh...*there's* the comfort. This is by far the most plush and luxurious bed I've ever been in. I starfish on the wide, soft surface and stretch out, arching my back like I'm giving my tits to God.

A moment later, the door clicks open, and Professor Charlton comes in, carrying my dress and shoes. Hopefully my panties as well.

She's no longer in that crazy tight dress. Now she's in a pink silk robe that's much looser, but somehow accentuates her curves even better. I've been hot for this woman since I first saw her, but seeing her like this—more relaxed and natural than ever before—makes her sexier than ever.

She places my stuff on a chair before settling her attention fully on me.

"Beautiful." Her voice is low and throaty, and I don't think she's talking about the room. And even though she's fired compliments my way, over and over, I still can't help but blush. In my head, I even retreat a little, waiting for the sting in the tail.

Professor Charlton closes the door behind her. I sit up, and my body sings with anticipation. I just want to watch her walk. See the way her body moves as she approaches me. It's like a Broadway show.

She seems to glide, her movements so smooth and fluid that she's barely touching the ground. It's like she's floating.

As she reaches the foot of the bed, she stops, facing me. She strokes her hands over one of my feet, and partway up my leg. When she brings them back down, she lifts a padded cuff and wraps it around my ankle.

Before she fastens it, she makes direct eye contact. Waiting. I don't trust my voice to work, but I also sense that a simple nod won't be enough.

"Y-yes, ma'am," I croak out, and Professor Charlton closes her eyes, an expression of pure bliss on her beautiful face.

"I'm so glad," she hums.

Chapter 5

SHE FASTENS THAT CUFF and then the other side. My belly is full of delicious prickling sensations, as I wonder exactly where this is leading. With my ankles secured to the bedposts, I'm held in place. I can sit up, and move my hands, but I can't get off the bed.

And I can't hide my slick, wet pussy from her, even if I want to.

The prof climbs on and straddles my hips. The sweet heat of her body kisses my skin, and her robe falls slightly open. I can tell she's naked beneath it and I let out a tiny little whine of anticipation that sounds more like a sob.

"Patience, cherie," Professor Charlton says, as she strokes my hair. It's so tender and sweet, but it just makes me hotter. I'm like a volcano about to erupt.

"Please, ma'am. Let me make you feel good."

"Hush, my little pudding." She leans down and kisses me, and it's a mix of passion and sweetness and raw animal desire. I feel like I could explode into a thousand pieces just from the taste of her mouth. "Embrace the restraints. Give me your agency for a short while. I will show you your worth."

"Oh, god, *please.*" I'm desperate, now. My obsessive brain has latched onto the possibility that I can connect with her even more deeply. That I could give her the same pleasure she's given me.

I reach for her but she catches my wrists, and does that magic trick where she caresses my pinch points with her thumbs.

"Patience," she repeats, and I just have to bite my lip and wait.

The prof kisses my nose, then my forehead. She glides forward until her magnificent tits are right there in front of my face. As she secures my hands in cuffs, one at a time, I drive my face between her breasts, kissing every part of her I can reach.

She lets out a soft *oh*, and then a long moan. I feel the sound, deep in her chest, even more than I hear it.

Then she pushes my head back and slips out of her robe. It's lightning quick and yet still feels like a tease. Like a show.

She's completely naked, and I can't help but stare. I want every single inch of her. I barely even think about what I'm doing as I try to reach for her. To take hold of those big, beautiful tits. To grasp her wide, fleshy hips. Stroke her belly. Drive my fingers up into her glistening pink cunt.

All of those thoughts fly through my head like squirrels on speed, and they tumble into space a split second later when the cuffs bite gently into my wrists. Once again, right in the spot where I pinch myself.

Professor Charlton smiles down at me, shaking her head. "I believe I cautioned you about patience, cherie?"

"But...but..." It's my strongest argument, and yet—surprise, surprise—it falls flat.

"Now, now, my little pudding. All is well."

Professor Charlton leans forward and glides her hand around the back of my head. She lifts me as she angles her breast forward, and I latch on to her hard nipple like it's oxygen. I suck on her sweet flesh and flick her with my tongue, moaning with relief.

"There, there, my baby," she hums, and holy fuck but that's wrong. And yet...oh, god, it's even hotter than when she calls me *cherie*, or her *little pudding*.

She feeds me her flesh and I suckle on it. I'm closer to this woman than I've ever been to anyone. I swear I can feel her heartbeat, and that mine is syncing up with it.

It's like a dream come true. I want to please her so badly. To give her everything.

"My good girl," she says, and those three short words hit me like a climax. I bite down on her bud without realizing I'm doing it.

Professor Charlton hisses with pain and eases herself back until she's sitting on my hips. She cups her boobs in her hands as the sweet heat of her inner thighs and her glorious pussy radiate over me. The warmth of her body, the musky scent of her arousal...it's all too much.

"Let me..." I don't finish my thought as I gaze up into her eyes. "Let me do it?"

She gazes down at me, her eyes sparkling. "Tell me what you want, my little pudding."

I swallow my hesitation and blurt out the truth. "I want to eat your pussy. Let me make you come."

Her eyes darken and her lips part with desire. "Oh, cherie." She lets out a long breath. "I normally don't allow it."

I shut my eyes, because her words sting me. The acknowledgement that, even though I'm new to all that we've done, she's been here before. Maybe she does it all the fucking time. And I must just be one in a sea of young and pretty—hopefully pretty—faces to her.

Still hiding behind my eyelids, I ask again. Beg, really. "Please?"

There's another moment of near silence, filled only by her breathing and mine. Then she shifts forward and positions her pussy over my mouth. "Just a taste, my good girl. A brief one, at that."

"But—"

"That is my rule."

I won't miss this chance, and I simply can't wait. I thrust my tongue up into her hot, wet cunt, and it's like an explosion for the senses. She's tangy and musky and sweet, and her fragrance spills over my skin as her flavor gushes across my tongue.

I clamp my mouth over her as if I've done this a thousand times, and it's so fucking natural and perfect and it's everything I wanted it to be. And it's all I can do not to drink her dry.

The professor lets out a moan that echoes through the room, and she grinds her pussy down over my face. This time she grips my hair, right on top of my head. She holds me in place as she rocks herself against me.

The restraints on my wrists give me a sense of security but they're also what's keeping me from touching her. From curling my hands over her thighs and holding her down until I can make her come.

Professor Charlton throws her other hand forward and grips the bedhead like it's the top of a cliff. I lash her with my tongue, seeking her clit. Virtually praying for her to come back down where I can slip that hot little button into my mouth and suck it all to hell.

She throws her head back and howls, still painting my face with her delicious juices. It's the hottest fucking thing I've ever seen. And it's all for me. *Because* of me.

As she comes, she presses right down on my mouth. She cries out again and again, and squeezes tight around my tongue as I drive it up into her. It's a powerful sensation, and I can barely breathe, but I don't want it to stop. I want her to come forever.

Professor Charlton eventually eases back, panting and trembling, and she releases her hold on my hair. I'm shaking too, but with desire and need.

She rolls off and sits on the bed beside me. But to my despair, she's facing away. Leaning her elbows on her knees and shaking her head.

Oh, god. Did she fake that orgasm? Was I that fucking terrible at eating pussy? "Please, Professor. I...I can do better. That was my first time ever—"

"No," she says, and it's almost a bark. It's so sharp and loud it makes me jump, and holy fuck but it's got me right back to the edge of tears. "No, my little pudding. You misunderstand me."

She turns and lies down on her front, pressing her bountiful body up against mine. Halfway across me, like she's a shield, and a comforter, and...well, like she's some kind of protective custody.

It's all too much for me. I shake my head as my vision blurs with tears.

"Oh, cherie. That was not meant to frighten you." She strokes my hair and my face, and my eyelids flutter closed.

She presses her sweet lips to mine, drinking herself from my mouth for a moment. "I...confess I didn't expect you to be so skillful. I broke two of my own rules with you, Giselle."

Professor Charlton is a ragged mess, now. Her hair is all wild, her makeup either worn away or smeared. And she's the most beautiful woman I've ever seen.

"You're...you're perfect."

"That's a sweet lie, my little pudding. And you are simply exquisite. It's rare that I...lose myself so quickly. So..."

"Please, go on?"

She brushes her fingers through my hair, gazing down at me with every ounce of her attention. "So completely."

I can't help but blush, and I hide my face in my shoulder.

"Sweet baby," she murmurs. "I consider myself enlightened. A woman of peace. Yet seeing you hide from praise like this, and my suspicion as to its origin...well, it makes me rather stabby."

I fling my head around, hearing her use that word. In that tone. It's as sharp as the metaphorical dagger she's talking about. But I'm not sure I'm brave enough to open up the discussion on all that. Not even sure I understand how I feel about the messed up relationships in my life. Including this one, if I'm honest.

"Well, my little pudding, it's late. You've derailed my plans in the most effusive fashion."

"I'm s—"

She silences my apology with nothing more than a tilt of her lovely head. "This is no bad thing, cherie. Perhaps I can be too rigid, at times."

Professor Charlton kisses my forehead, then sits up and removes my cuffs. I don't know what to say or do, so I just watch her work. When the blood flows more easily to my limbs I swim in a small burst of euphoria. As if she's taken me apart and reassembled me in a more fitting way.

My professor once again takes my hands and lifts them to her face. She massages my wrists with a gossamer touch, and kisses my pinch points. "Are you okay to drive?"

I bite down on the pleading response that leaps into mind. To let me stay here with her. In her bed.

But there was no promise of any of that. A sleepover? That sort of thing is obviously beneath a late-30s college professor. And I'm a fucking idiot for thinking this is more than it really is.

I'm a scratching post for her kitty. That's my role, here. If I see anything that looks deeper than that on her face, it's because I'm putting it there.

"I...yes, I can manage."

Professor Charlton nods, and rises from the bed. "I will see you in class, cherie."

Her tone is warm and caring, but her words are a clear dismissal.

I scramble from the bed and pull on my dress, then grab my phone and purse and stumble out of the room. Too numb for tears or goodbyes.

Professor Charlton follows me to the front door. I get the feeling it's so she can be sure I actually get the fuck out of her house.

"Giselle," she says, just before I close the door, and I pause without looking back. "We must keep this between ourselves."

"Well, duh."

I'm not looking at her, but I can imagine her expression tightening out of annoyance. "And you will dress modestly on Thursday, cherie."

I purse my lips so hard they must be white. Does she really think she can order me around when she's clearly done with me?

Do *I* truly think I'll refuse her?

"Yes, ma'am."

END OF BOOK 2

Aftermath

Book 3

Chapter 1

I'm STILL PISSED AT Professor Charlton. Using me for her pleasure is one thing, and I guess I kinda signed up for that. I mean, I have no problem with someone taking me to orgasm multiple times. Duh.

It's that little fucking pantomime she put on that was ridiculous. Claiming she never lets her little sex toys eat her out, and then riding my face like it was a prize filly. How fucking stupid does she think I am?

Worse still, when she got done with me, what the fuck was with her sending me away like I'm nothing more than an indentured servant? And to top it all off, still having the fucking gall to tell me what to wear the next time she sees me.

I fucking *hate* her. At least, every minute I'm not pining for her, that is. Wishing I could bury my fingers and tongue in that woman's perfect pussy, over and over. Desperate to have her do the same to me. Yearning for her to help me explore that sense of pure freedom and release that came to life within me the moment she attached those restraints.

It's so damn hard to concentrate on the road as I drive in. I keep remembering the blissful agony when Professor Charlton landed those sharp, blistering smacks on my ass. How, for just a moment, it let my mind go still and actually focus. And it makes me crave more of it. The sweet pain, and the flow-on effect it might have on my squirrel brain.

As I navigate the traffic, I squirm in my seat. It's been a whole day and night since I saw the prof, and I'm jonesing something fucking fierce. Even if I only get to see her, and listen to her voice, I think that might be enough. Fuck knows if I even want to talk to her, let alone do anything physical.

My fingers itch with the desire to pinch my wrist, and suddenly I can't remember doing that at all since I made Professor Carlton come on my mouth.

At least if I sit back and soak up her presence today, I can store it in my spank banks. Take it home with me and beat my poor little clit to death in the shower.

Christ, I'm so fucking desperate for her touch I can barely breathe. I just need to get through class, and then I can flee into the bathroom and grind myself to a quick climax. Just for fucking maintenance purposes.

Professor Charlton is already in the room as I enter, and my belly flutters with the familiar sensation of my heart in my throat. She's sitting at her desk, writing on a pad of paper. But as I walk in, she glances up and raises her perfectly shaped eyebrow. The one she uses to cut my confidence to pieces every single time.

When she scans me from head to toe, she seems...well, not exactly pleased, but I suppose more like mollified. And why the hell am I even worried how she feels about *any-thing?* She's used me up and tossed me away, right?

Still, I've done as she told me to and dressed conservatively, even though I shouldn't have. I should've turned up in a fucking bra and thong, just to show her she's not the boss of me. Except she fucking is, and she and I both know it.

A trip back to the thrift store yesterday yielded church-girl gold. A knee length sky blue summer dress with a high neckline. It even has fucking sleeves, although they're pretty short. It's tight as hell up top, but the skirt puffs out a little around my hips.

It was so tempting to mismatch the dress with a pair of floral patterned Crocs, but I resisted. Just some casual strappy sandals to complete the look. I even have my hair under control—sort of. A tight ponytail, tied with a scarf that matches my dress. Christ, I feel like I'm part of a damn youth group choir or something.

I have no idea what the hell is wrong with me. Why I'm dressing like this for someone who doesn't give a shit. But I guess it's like the old saying goes—you can't fix stupid. And nothing makes me stupid like sex-on-legs Professor Charlton.

I take a seat right up the back of the room, behind everyone else. It's basically a passive-aggressive protest on my part. And a self-punishment, I guess, since I'm so much further away from the prof. As usual, she's all buttoned down and crisp. Neat lines and impeccable makeup. Not a hair that dares to be out of place.

She turns to face the class and speaks clearly, but I barely hear a word. I'm just transfixed by her every move and expression. She's so fucking perfect, and I'm so fucking needy.

And I'm still pissed at her. That hasn't changed.

At least I can get through this class without having to talk to her, or interact with her in any way. I just have to keep my head down and my thoughts to myself.

When the class finally finishes, I close my eyes and congratulate myself for making it all the way to the end. For avoiding eye contact with that irresistible bitch, and keeping a steely focus. I mean, mostly. I'm sure I only daydreamed about Professor Charlton tying me up maybe a half-dozen times. Another 8 or 9 times fantasizing about being soundly spanked by her. Oh, and a few hundred times picturing her immaculate face down between my thighs.

Jesus, I am so fucking wet. I hope I haven't left a patch on this dress. Why the hell didn't I wear black?

Professor Charlton dismisses us all with her usual *goodbye, ragamuffins*. I'm still too nervous to stand, but everyone else starts filing out.

"Oh, and for an ongoing study I'm conducting, I shall require a volunteer." Most of the other students pause and glance at each other. I sit frozen in place, and I know it's in misplaced rage as much as fear of the unknown. What confuses me is that the rage is borne from pure jealousy at the thought of some other student working closely with Professor Sexypants.

"Ah, thank you, Miss Belmont. I appreciate you putting your trust in me."

What? I didn't raise my hand. Didn't call out. Fuck, I've barely managed to take a breath since she dismissed us.

"Everyone else may go. Miss Belmont, I'll need to give you a briefing. Please join me in my office."

I've been crazy keyed up throughout the class. So much so that I don't think I took down a single note. Now she's speaking directly to me, and I know I'm about to be all alone with her...yeah, my legs aren't gonna hold up to that.

I might have to roll down the stairs to her. That is, if I don't just drizzle like a spill of hot liquid.

When all my classmates have left, Professor Charlton leans her lovely round ass on the lecture hall desk. She takes off her glasses, crosses her arms, and slays me with that sexy eyebrow once again.

"Miss Belmont?"

"What?"

All the prof does in reaction to my petulant reply is to kink her head an inch to the side, and it blows the last of my resistance away. I struggle to my feet and stumble down until I'm standing right before her. It takes a mammoth effort to keep from dropping to my knees.

"W–what do you need, ma'am?"

"My office, cherie," she murmurs. It's so quiet that nobody outside could hear her, and yet it hits me like a soft, wet pillow. She's running hot and cold, and I don't think my mind or my body can take it. And still, I follow her, even

closing and locking the door the moment she orders me to.

Chapter 2

"GISELLE, I AM MOST pleased with you."

I squeeze my hands into fists and I'm sure I must look like a spoiled brat. "Why should I care what you—"

"Now, now, my little pudding. Take care."

I slam my eyes closed and screw my face up in frustration. All I want is to yell at her. Tell her to go fuck herself. And then she goes and calls me her *little pudding* again and my stupid brain—or at least, my pussy—melts. And takes my self-control with it.

"I don't know what you want, Professor."

"Turn around please, cherie."

I do as I'm told. As I always do with her. As I probably always will.

Professor Charlton rests her hands on my shoulders, and stupid me, I wish I'd worn a strapless dress instead. Just to feel her, skin to skin. I'm at war inside my own head. I absolutely love giving over my self-control to this goddess, and yet I fucking hate how much I love it.

The prof pulls back on me, just lightly, until my back is resting against her chest. Her warm breath cascades past my ear and down the side of my neck as she eases her hands inward.

After five seconds that feel like five years, she traces her fingertips up and down the sides of my neck, and I swear every single inch of my skin comes alive with goose bumps. I hold my breath long enough to hurt, and when I let it out, it becomes a whimper.

"You exceeded my expectations, Giselle."

"Huh?"

"I feared you would offer up some pointless resistance after the way I dismissed you. That you'd rebel against my directive *vis-à-vis* your attire."

"You..." I swallow as I try to gather my thoughts. "It was a test?"

"Mmm...it's more akin to a game." She kisses the side of my neck and I can't hold in the moan of relief and pleasure. Then she presses her lips to my ear and whispers. "You like games, don't you?"

"Yesss..." I sound like I've sprung a leak.

"Good girl."

Oh, fuck. Those words send a thrill of lightning through me, and I shiver uncontrollably. "Are we...are we playing now?"

She lets out a slow, steady breath. "Sweet girl, I'm always playing."

Professor Charlton wraps her hand around my pony-tail and draws back on it. Just lightly, not enough to hurt—yet—and she leans my head back against her shoulder. She places her other hand on my belly and I jump in surprise. Slowly, like a glacier, she glides that hand up my body, between my breasts, and on to my throat.

"Mm. You are like velvet, cherie."

"Thank—"

That's as far as I get before Professor Charlton tightens her grip, hard enough to block my air. My knees quiver and threaten to give way, and if not for this tall, voluptuous goddess holding me up, I'd simply collapse to the floor. I writhe against her body, my eyes bulging in fear as I struggle for breath, and yet I'm not actually trying to escape. I'm just trying to process the onslaught of pleasure.

The prof kisses my cheek, then takes the skin between her teeth. She bites down so lightly it won't even leave a mark, but it's a sign of exactly what she could do. The sweetness of pain that she could inflict on me so easily. And I swear, I'm close to coming just from the thought of it.

Finally, she releases her grip, and I suck in a lungful of air. My breath rasps in and out, and from somewhere in the dark recesses of my mind, three key words tumble out of my mouth.

"Thank you, ma'am…"

"Oh, my. You are such a good girl, cherie." She massages my throat, and my body practically sings with the sensation. It's so tender and caring. On the surface, it's a massive contrast to what she's just done, and yet already I can see it's like two opposite branches of the same tree. "Now, be my little pudding, and lift your skirt for me."

"Ma'am?"

"I confess I'm suspicious that you so readily followed my directions. I suspect I shall find some rather racy knickers beneath this splendid but quite orthodox dress."

"I promise, Professor. You won't."

"Indeed?" She traces her soft lips up and down the side of my neck, her breath caressing my skin and her scent caressing my senses. "Show me."

Oh, god. I'm in so much trouble, and it's magnificent. Rather than bending and taking my neck away from this woman's sensuous mouth, I press my palms to my thighs and drag upward. The prof's breathing grows heavier with every slow inch I reveal.

And it stops completely for a moment when I reveal that I'm not wearing any panties at all. Her grip on my ponytail tightens, and she twists that hand, bringing a burst of sweet pain to my scalp.

"I should be disappointed in you, cherie," she murmurs between soft kisses up and down my neck. "And yet you have both defied me and exceeded my expectations, all at once."

"I aim to please, ma'am."

She chuckles. "You are a natural, my little pudding."

Professor Charlton places her hand on my bare hip, and I suck in a breath that's all surprise. When she glides her fingers in against my mound, I bite into my bottom lip and make fists in the loose fabric of my raised skirt.

Then, when the prof slides her soft fingers through my hot, wet groove, I arch backward against her. Pleasure floods my mind and body as Professor Charlton drives two fingers up inside me. It's almost like it was that first time, here in her office. Me leaning on her, desperate for the support she gives me. Her driving me fucking crazy with just the touch of her hand, the heat of her body.

"Come for me, cherie," she moans, straight into my ear. "Come hard for mama..."

Oh, god. The world suddenly goes blindingly white as broad fists of pleasure punch through my body. I screw my eyes closed and cry out with my release, and Professor Charlton coos and sighs as I coat her hand with my juices.

"Good girl. Oh, my sweet, good girl."

She pumps her fingers in and out of my hot little cunt, and I'm still coming. It's like she's drawing out my climax, stretching it into an endless stream of bliss.

Finally, she withdraws her fingers and pauses for a moment. I figure she's about to kiss me and maybe send me away again. Like she has before.

Instead, she spins us on the spot and pushes until my belly presses against the edge of her desk. She pulls the blue scarf from around my ponytail and my hair cascades free. Then she sweeps her desk clear and pushes on the center of my back, bending me forward.

Oh, god. I've just finished coming and already I'm all keyed up again.

"Hands on your back, cherie," she murmurs, and I do exactly as she says, crossing them at the wrists. Professor Charlton wraps my scarf around my elbows and partway down my forearms before she secures it with some kind of knot. It's taken next to no time and frankly, I'm blown away by her skill. Maybe she was a girl scout or something.

The stretch in my shoulders is invigorating and carries just a little pain with it. And when she grabs the top of my skirt and yanks it up over my ass, I let out a tiny moan of desire.

"Now, my little pudding. You've been a very good girl, so I'm going to reward you."

"Thank you, ma'am."

"But you've also been a very, very bad girl. So I need to punish you."

"Ohh...y–yes, ma'am."

Chapter 3

THE SHARP IMPACT OF her hand on my bare ass stings like fire, but it's not really pain. Or at least, it's not the kind I've known it in the past. This is what pain evolves into when it grows up.

Again and again, Professor Charlton lands sweet, stinging spanks on my ass. Every one just a little bit away from the last. One side and the other. None of them all that hard, but the constant stream of them keeps the pain level simmering so fucking nicely. And I jump with every impact, and I roll my hips and squirm as pleasure floods my body, and arousal floods my cunt.

I'm lost to the sensation of it all, and I'm not even sure if I'm crying or laughing. Moaning or wailing. All I know is that this is exactly what I want and need. And fuck, but I wish I could be like this all the time. Just an object of pure pleasure for this incredible woman.

After a few more slaps, Professor Charlton stops. She leans down and kisses my ear, and then whispers to me. "Pink is such a lovely color on you, my little pudding."

"Thank you, mama." Oh, fuck. Why does it feel even better to call her that than to call her ma'am? Same letters, just a different order. My brain is one fucked up little squirrel, for sure. But the prof said it herself. It's a game. If she's always playing, then why can't I?

She chuckles and strokes her hand down my spine, making me arch like a cat. "You are a delight, my girl. And so very sweet."

Professor Charlton kneels behind me and kisses the flesh she's just tortured. From one side to the other, and down to the backs of my thighs.

"Perfect," she moans, and then she glides her tongue up and down my hot, aching slit. Her hums and moans vibrate deeply into me, and the slick, sticky sounds of her mouth on my pussy are nearly as hot as the sensations she's giving me.

Professor Charlton grips my tortured ass cheeks and squeezes, igniting a new wall of pain as she drives her tongue deep inside me. I hold my breath as the pressure builds in my core.

When she finally sends me over the edge, I come with a cry that sounds more like a sob. Tears stream down my face, and I know it's not just the ecstasy of the moment, or the ache in my flesh. It's all the emotions of the last few days. The anger, the hurt, the desire.

The love.

I come down from the sheer stratospheric high I'm on, struggling for breath. The cold wood of the desk has grown warm beneath me, and my breath saws in and out like I've run a marathon.

Only after a few moments does it hit me what I've just told myself. The word I used.

Love? Fucking hell. This woman has occupied pretty much my every thought for weeks now. She's made me come harder than I ever have before. I readily admit I have a weird obsession with her.

But *love?*

She's done this to me. Blurring lines all over the goddamn place. Calling me all those cute names to make me warm to her. Calling me her *sweet baby*, and herself *mama?* Jesus. Trigger city.

And suddenly, I no longer feel open and free. I feel trapped and vulnerable and completely transparent. I struggle against the scarf binding my arms, and though I try to ask the prof to free me, nothing that comes out of my mouth sounds like a recognizable word.

Thankfully, she understands just fine, and releases the knot. I fling my arms out and slap my palms down onto the desk, as if an earthquake has just hit and I'm striving not to be shaken off my perch. Swallowed up by the earth.

"Giselle?" Her voice is low and calm, and it reaches me like a buoy in the ocean. "Talk to me, cherie."

I stand straight and push my skirt back down. Adjust my sleeves and especially the front of my dress, where my tits have fought themselves halfway out. Covering my body like I wish I could mask my feelings off from this woman.

But I can't find the way to express my thoughts. Not right now. I wipe my cheeks dry and shake my head.

Professor Charlton walks around and takes her seat, and for a moment I picture myself following her. Climbing into her lap and curling up into a ball. Calling her *mama* again and having her call me *sweet baby*.

It doesn't take a genius to see what's going on here. The void in my life that this woman has not only recognized, but has fit herself into. Normally, I'd feel played or tricked, but with Professor Charlton, I honestly don't sense any danger. Maybe that in itself should set off fucking alarm bells.

"You are everything I hoped you would be, Giselle. And more. You will be a perfect participant in my study."

Oh, yeah. That. It's supposedly the whole reason I've stayed back today.

"There really is a study?"

"Of course, my little pudding." She pulls her mouth into a tiny smile and winks at me. "Why, did you think it was a ruse, merely so I could get into your non-existent knick-ers?"

I lower my gaze in embarrassment, because yeah, that's exactly what I thought. Before I can stop myself, I reach over and pinch the skin of my wrist.

"Tut tut, cherie. I'd hoped we'd moved past that." The professor reaches down and picks her notepad up from where she swept it onto the floor. "Now, about that study."

Then she writes something down, tears it off and folds it. She holds it out to me, but when I reach for it, she seems to have second thoughts. She frowns and pulls it back out of my reach. "Oh, sweet girl. I do fear you might not be ready for this next step."

"I'm ready. Well, I mean, I hope." I swallow and shake my head like a puzzle, hoping it rolls all the little steel balls into the holes. "I trust your judgement. And I trust *you*, Professor Charlton."

She narrows her eyes, and I hope I haven't come across as too desperate. Bad enough I just used the fucking L word inside my head. How the fuck can I be spouting words like *trust* already? This morning I thought she'd tossed me away like a broken toy.

"My good girl." She hands me the note with a smile. "The time and the address are on that note. The dress code is neat casual. I do hope to see you."

Chapter 4

WHAT AM I EVEN doing here? I'm beyond nervous, and I have been since this afternoon. I couldn't even wrap my head around what qualifies as neat casual, so I'm in another thrift store outfit. Pencil skirt and white blouse, with killer heels that are only a half size too big for me. Really, I just feel as if I'm copying Professor Charlton's look, but at least I have underwear on this time.

The address leads me to an upscale apartment building. One that has a security guard stationed at the front door. I feel like I'm about to attend a private party or something. Only my belly tingles as if I'm really crashing it, rather than being an invited guest.

When the security guard asks me who I'm here with, I give Professor Charlton's name, and he waves me through. The elevator ride to the 14th floor takes forever, and I can barely keep myself still. I regret now that I didn't take a little swig of something before I left my place, but my driving is already dodgy when I'm fully sober.

When the elevator stops and the doors slide open, it's straight into the apartment itself. Classy beyond anything I've ever known. I find myself in a large living room that's dimly lit but warm looking. Dark wooden walls with sparse furniture. To my surprise, there's a mid-size crowd of people milling about and chatting in small groups.

"Miss Belmont?"

Professor Charlton approaches me from the left, and I'm struck by how stunning she is. A tight black dress hugs her curves, flowing all the way down to her ankles. Not a single line anywhere, making me feel certain she's naked beneath it. Her makeup is immaculate, and her hair flows freely down to her shoulders, unlike it ever does in class. It makes me desperate to run my fingers through it.

I'm such a fucking mess, and this is just the start of it.

"Yes, Professor Charlton."

"Thank you for coming. Please, let me introduce you around." She leads me around the room, introducing me to several other people. All older than me, and quite a few older than the professor. Singles and couples, and interestingly enough, more women than men. It's all kind of overwhelming, and I'm sure I won't remember any of their names.

Once we've made a lap of the room, and my brain's been utterly filled beyond overflowing, Professor Charlton takes me into a small private room.

"So," I say. "You know a lot of other professors."

"Who said they were professors, cherie?"

"They aren't? Then...who...?"

I reach for my wrist, but Professor Charlton takes hold of my hands. "Relax, my little pudding. They will adore you."

There's no doubt my confusion is all over my face, but the prof just smiles and glides her hands up my arms, coming to rest on my shoulders. When she leans in and kisses my forehead, I automatically put my arms around her waist and pull her closer. With my head against her big boobs, it's as close to home as I've known in a long time.

"What is this place? Ma'am?"

"It's...well," she says, and then pauses. I've never known her to be so coy. "This is my ex-husband's ex-apartment. My divorce settlement was rather generous."

"Oh." She told me she's not a lesbian, but I guess I just thought she hated labels. Knowing she's been married—to a man—has my belly tied up in knots, and I really don't know why.

She draws back like she hasn't just made origami with my brain, and she takes a deep breath. "Giselle, I need to explain. I said I'm conducting a study, but I confess, that's more my pet name for it."

I don't know how to react. It's hard enough to even process the words she's saying.

"Cherie, I see you in a way you seem unwilling or unable to see yourself. The shadows you hide within, and the parts of your nature you apparently believe are somehow wrong."

Once again, she intercepts my hands before I can pinch myself.

"Please, professor…"

"Sweet baby. Your needs, your cravings…you're permitted to feel them. They're important to me, but to you they're utterly vital."

I can only stare at her as she completely strips away all the defenses I've put up over the years. How does this woman see me better than my own mother can? Better even than I see myself?

A moment of silence passes, and then Professor Charlton continues. "You fascinate me, Miss Belmont. I have a desire to help you find your way. To guide you into exploring this side of yourself."

"My lesbian side?"

For a moment, she pauses, and I'm certain a quiver of sensation must have rolled through her body. She kinks her hips to the side as she licks her gorgeous lips. The simple belief that I've affected her gives me a burst of cocky strength, and I double down.

"We don't need a crowd of strangers for me to explore that, prof. You just hike your dress up and I will fucking devour your sweet cunt right here and now."

I know it's a gamble, trying to take the wheel like this. Spouting coarse language like a piece of half-chewed trailer trash. Just like when I'm driving, I can't help being a jittery person. Much more reactive than active.

"In good time, cherie," Professor Charlton says, stroking the backs of her fingers down my cheek. "But first, I wish to help you explore your inner exhibitionist."

"My inner what, now?"

The prof walks around behind me, smooth like a fucking ballerina. Every time we're alone together, she always ends up behind me. Like a wall to lean on. Or a cross to bear.

She reaches around and works open the top button of my blouse. "Come now, cherie," she says, then kisses my neck. I never even knew that was my weakness, but somehow, the prof discovered it straight away. And she uses it against me every fucking time. "I know you. There is nothing you desire more than to be seen. Truly, wholeheartedly *seen*."

By the time she's finished speaking, my blouse is open, and she slides it off me. A few seconds pass and my bra follows. She glides to her knees, kissing a meandering path down my spine as she goes. A moment later, she has my pencil skirt and my panties down around my ankles. One by one, she slides my shoes off, leaving me standing in a strange room in a strange place, without a single stitch of clothing on.

"Such a beauty," she moans, then kisses the exposed and still raw skin of my ass. One cheek, and then the other. "This will be such a treat."

"W–what's happening, mama?" Christ. Did I really just call her that again?

"With your permission, my little pudding, I'm showing you off. Your beauty and your power."

"I don't understand."

She leads me over to the door and opens it a crack. "Look through there. To the right. You see the low stage?"

I nod, not trusting my voice to actually work.

"That is where I shall take you, Giselle. Really, truly *take you*. I shall strip you of all pretenses and govern you the way only I can. And I will not let up until you climax."

"But they'll all...I mean, everyone will see me. Us."

"Oh, they will see you, as you shine like a star for us all. You are the artwork. I am merely the frame."

"Oh, god." I'm instantly both overwhelmed and aroused as hell. This is like tough love swimming lessons. Tossing me in at the deep end and expecting me to find some way—any way—to keep from going under.

And yet, I don't think I've ever been more excited in my life.

Chapter 5

She takes me by the shoulders and turns me to face her. "You are strong, cherie. You are momentous." She leans in and kisses me, and it's like a tidal wave of sensations. Her soft lips, her breath, the sweet taste of her lipstick. It all swamps me and draws me in. Her lips are still tickling mine when she speaks again. "You are *mine*."

There's such a fierce hunger in her voice, and it has my breath trembling. "Yes, mama."

She smiles and caresses my cheek with her fingertips. "Sweet baby." She leads me toward the door. "Just one more thing."

Professor Charlton heads over to a cabinet at the wall. She comes back holding what looks like a leather strip. It's only as she fastens it around my neck that I realize it's a collar. With a fucking leash.

"What the—"

"Shh. It's part of the show. You're such a natural, sweet baby. I know you'll nail it."

It's clear I'm little more than a praise-slut. Because anytime the prof gives me a boost like that, it works like crazy. I actually believe I'm capable of anything she tells me.

"Ready, my little pudding?"

"Ready, mama."

"Good girl."

Professor Charlton pushes the door open and leads me out into the room. The crowd is now all seated on the floor around the stage, and even in the low light, I'm certain their eyes glow. Like wolves in the night.

We step up onto the stage, and only then do bright lights come on above us. With my pale skin, I must be fucking glowing in the dark, and I can see what the prof meant before. In her long black dress, she blends into the dark wall behind us, leaving all the focus on me. My naked body.

I'm completely exposed, and yet I'm flying, with a sense of elation beyond anything I've known before. My pussy is suddenly a witch's cauldron, and it's simmering away. It's not like I'm anywhere near climax, exactly. I'm just...heightened.

Professor Charlton gives her leash a short, soft tug, and it has me gasping in surprise and standing taller. She follows up by placing her hand under my chin, tilting my head until I'm arching backward at the waist. I sense it's a display of trust. My entire soft underbelly—throat, tits, abdomen and pussy—are all out on display to this crowd of strangers.

And they're all staring at me and murmuring their approval. It's like a sexy dream come true, and I'm so wet and hot that I'm certain I'm dripping onto the stage.

"That's my good little pudding," Professor Charlton whispers, and I can barely hold back the moan that rises in my throat. She leans in and kisses my lips, and I'm suddenly overwhelmed by the desire to kiss her back. To turn and take her mouth with mine.

She pulls back and gives me a knowing smile. "Later, cherie."

Oh, god.

The prof walks around behind me, taking hold of my elbow. As she gives her leash another little tug, she pulls my arm. I follow the hint, turning my back to the near invisible audience. Exposing more of me to their hungry gaze, and I swear I can feel every one of them tracing my body with just their eyes. And it's thrilling.

Professor Charlton glides her hand down my spine, making me shiver and arch like a cat. She reaches my ass and slides her fingers down between my cheeks. It's like she's claiming me in front of everyone, and I'm sure I hear someone in the crowd moan in response. The prof glides on until just the tips of her fingers are kissing my wet and needy slit, and then glides back up to the cheek of my ass.

She kneads my flesh, then lands a sharp slap that rolls through me. A few low moans and sharp gasps from the audience tell me they like what they see. The dance of my flesh to the beat of my lover's hand.

She strikes again, and this time it's louder, but not as sharp. More pleasure than pain. Already I can tell Professor Charlton has the touch of a concert pianist when it comes to spanking. She's showing off her skills for the crowd—and for me—and it's getting me insanely hot.

The prof follows up the brief session of smacks by stroking the heated skin. She tightens the pressure on my leash and whispers "hands and knees" to me, and though I want to obey her, immediately, I'm held in check by shame. It's only residual, and I thought I was over it, but there it is. As hot as it is to be standing naked in front of all these strangers, the thought of mooning them has me paralyzed in fear.

It's not even simply the fact they'll see every private inch of my body. It's more the fact they'll see just how fucking wet the professor makes me. How weak I am for her. They won't just see my ass and my cunt...they'll know my secrets.

"I see," Professor Charlton says, reaching her hand out toward the audience. "We finally reach an impasse."

Finally? What is she talking—

My thoughts are completely obliterated when she brings her hand back into my line of sight. Holding something made of black leather. It looks almost like a flat baseball bat.

Oh, fuck. It's a paddle.

And suddenly, I'm taken back to the lecture hall, a few lessons back. What the prof was talking about. *Looking at the effect pain can have in eliciting obedience. And the subsequent use of that obedience in the seeking of worldly pleasures.*

I didn't understand her, then. All I knew was it sounded hot as fuck. I'm not sure I fully understand it now, either, because I can't tell which of us is getting more pleasure from the moment. Who's the one who's truly seeking?

The moment Professor Charlton strokes the leather paddle gently over my ass, I realize I've been waiting for this. Not literally to be paddled naked in front of an entire group of people, but something like this; both confronting and cathartic. And now that it's here, I can barely think straight.

Professor Charlton turns the paddle until just one point of it is pressed to my skin. She traces the rounded heart shape of my ass, one side and the other, and I'm certain I hear murmurs of appreciation from the audience. Then, without warning, she gives me a hard smack right across both cheeks that leaves me gasping.

The sharp stinging sensation floods my senses and blurs my vision. It takes all my willpower to keep from crying out.

But I stand tall.

"Oh, my," Professor Charlton says, her voice a molten sound of desire. "Cherie..."

She lands a second whipping blow, and my body leaps like she's electrocuted me. My nipples are so hard I swear they're straining for freedom, and the collar bites into my throat. The pain is delicious, and it's like a volcano erupting in my head. The heat of sensation drizzles down from my mind and through my body. It burns away my pride and my stubbornness. More importantly, it utterly obliterates my shame.

Suddenly, I don't care about any of that. All I want is more. More pain, more pleasure.

More professor.

And I get it. She rains down a flurry of spanks on my ass, and with each one, the sensation seems to flow into my pussy like a river. It's as if my ass is a conduit, and the pain is simply a means to an end.

It's all so fucking hot that I can barely breathe, and I'm not sure how long I can take it. But Professor Charlton doesn't let up. She continues to paddle my ass, and every time she strikes me, she follows it up with a quick burst of praise.

"Mmm, that's it, cherie."

"My good girl."

"Mama can't wait to kiss it better, my sweet baby."

Chapter 6

THE LAST ONE BREAKS me, and finally I obey her. I drop to my knees and prop my ass up, my legs miles apart. And even though every one of those strangers can see my glistening slit, and the arousal that's drizzling down my inner thighs, it doesn't matter. They're nothing and nobody.

The only thing that matters is that Professor Charlton can see everything I would normally hide. All my holes. All my secrets.

"Yes," the professor says, a whispered cry of triumph. She tightens the leash and cuts off my air, then tosses the paddle away. She drives her fingers down the crease of my soaking wet cunt. When she pinches my clit, it's like I've been shot from below.

"Oh, fuck!" I cry out as she sends me hurtling toward climax. "I'm coming! Fuck!"

Professor Charlton gives the leash another sharp tug as she thrusts three fingers inside my hot little cunt. I come so hard I see stars. The audience gasps and moans, and I know they're enjoying the show. It's like being in a porn film, except it's real.

I don't know how long I'm spaced out for on the sheer bliss of that enormous climax. There's low sound all around me—voices, footsteps—but nothing that really takes hold inside my head.

When I finally come back into my own mind, I'm still on my knees, my face and chest against the floor. Professor Charlton's stroking my pussy with one hand and still holding my leash with the other.

"Shh," she says. "There's my good little pudding."

"Ohhh..." With my orgasm now over, I suddenly feel far too exposed. I fling my eyes open and try to get up, but the prof stops me.

"They're all gone, cherie," she says. "We're alone."

"What...what was this, mama?"

She pulls her luscious bottom lip inward and bites down on it for a moment. Then she puffs out a short sigh. "It's a social club, cherie. For want of a more accurate term. And it's an integral factor in facilitating my divorce."

Her tone is sharp and so I sense the matter's closed, at least for now. "M–may I stand, ma'am?"

"Of course."

Professor Charlton helps me to my feet and draws me into her embrace. I practically melt against her, the curves of her body filling the gaps of mine. She kisses the top of my head and whispers words of praise and encouragement, and I'm overwhelmed with the sensation.

It's like a warm blanket wrapping around me, but it's so much more. So much better. It's her praise, and her acceptance. I don't even want to risk thinking about that other thing. *Ell owe vee ee.* And whether she could ever feel it for me.

But there's one thing I *do* need her to feel.

"Please, Professor Charlton?"

"What is it, Giselle?"

I take a half step backward and press my hand to the front of her dress. Right over her pussy. "Let me?"

"Miss Belmont," she says, and it's clear she's trying to distance herself. Turn me back into her student, instead of her...well, whatever it is I am.

"Let me pleasure you? Please..." I pull out the only thing I can think of that might swing things my way. "Please, Alicia?"

She slams her eyes shut and turns her face half away. I take advantage of the moment and push firmly against her, forcing my professor back against the wall. It's so unlike me to even seem assertive, let alone being literally pushy like this. And the moment Professor Charlton thuds against the dark wood, she whips her eyes open in clear surprise. She even drops the leash.

"Giselle..."

I hold my finger over my lips, but it's a request, not an order. She's still in charge, and I'm just seeing what I can get away with. I kink my head upward and kiss her beautiful lips, and she parts for me instantly. Together we sing a wordless tune of moans and sighs, as I drive my tongue inside her mouth.

Usually, Professor Charlton is all about control. Somehow, I seem to have found a way to sidestep it, at least for a moment. And while she's all soft and malleable, I glide to my knees and take hold of her long dress. There's no time for subtlety or hesitation, so I haul it up from her ankles until it's over her waist.

And I'm absolutely mesmerized by the sheer beauty of her bare pussy. Even more than last time. The rich fragrance of her arousal has my skin tingling with need, and I fall forward as if I'm drunk. And maybe I am, even though I haven't touched a drop of alcohol.

Professor Charlton's sweet tang washes over my tongue as I press my mouth up against her slick, wet lips. She gazes down into my eyes and I swear I've never seen her look so fucking soft. So wet.

So vulnerable.

It's like we're seeing each other for the first time.

She reaches out and strokes my cheek with the back of her fingers, and then tangles them in my hair. Her touch is gentle and reassuring, and yet she still holds me in place. She's in control, even if she doesn't feel like it right now. I scrabble around until I have a hold on the leash, and I hand it up to her.

Professor Charlton moans with pleasure as she takes hold of the leash and pulls it tight. I drive my tongue up inside her hot cunt, and the taste of her explodes in my head. She's sweet and smoky, and it bites like a habanero. It's a symphony of flavors in my mouth. And the longer I drink from her, the more her grip on my hair tightens.

Finally, Professor Charlton lets out a cry that fills the room, and she comes all over my face. A fresh burst of her flavor fills my senses, and the high whining sounds of her release fill my soul. She grinds her hips forward and back, mashing her sweet cunt across my face, and I turn my head one way and the other as I bathe in her.

The prof slides down the wall and lands on her perfect ass. She removes my collar and tosses it across the room, then pulls me into a kiss that's more violent and ravenous than any she's given me before. She bites into my lips and my tongue as she rolls me down onto my back.

I raise my leg between hers and she grinds her slick pussy against my thigh, harder and harder. She grips my wrists and slams both hands down on the floor of the stage. The sheer weight of her ignites a dull pain right where I usually pinch, and she raises herself to glare down at me like I've done something wrong.

There's a fire in her eyes that's beyond reason, and for the first time, I'm truly scared. Not that she'll hurt me. I welcome the kind of pinpoint blissful agony she gives me.

What I'm scared of is that she's seeing something in me that reminds her of someone else. Someone who's fucked her over.

Once again, it's like she can read my mind. Professor Charlton relaxes her grip on my arms, and the fierce heat in her expression slides almost instantly back into a soft calm. All except the hard frown creasing her brow.

She shakes her head and sits back, releasing my wrists. A moment later, she stands and turns away from me.

"Giselle," she says. "You cannot be here."

"W–what?" Fuck. I thought we were just getting started. God, I'm ready for so much more. I swear she was about to take me to bed and fuck me for the rest of the fucking night.

Instead, she closes herself off once more. Smooths her dress back down over her thighs. "You need to leave. You're not...this is not..."

"Not what?"

"Proper." She shakes her head and turns her back. "Just go, Miss Belmont. Please."

I don't have time to process what's happening. She doesn't look back at me as she steps off the low stage, half stumbling on unsteady legs. She takes a moment to regather herself and then walks up the hallway. I hear the soft sound of a door closing and a deep, cold chasm opens up inside me.

With nothing else to do, I retrieve my clothes and dress myself hesitantly. Half-hoping she'll come running back and tackle me to the floor just to stop me from leaving.

All the way back to my car, I keep that flame burning. And once I'm in the driver's seat, I know it's not happening. For all the heat between us, once again, she's gone cold. Frozen me out. And I don't know why.

How can I fix things when I don't know what I've done wrong?

I struggle to get the key into the ignition with my trembling hands. Just before I start the engine, my phone pings, and I leap on it like a hungry lion on a wildebeest.

> *Tomorrow night, cherie. Formal but sexy attire. I will text you the time and place.*

It's not an apology, but then I'm not sure if I'm due one or not. Whatever it is, I'll take it.

Yes, ma'am. <

END OF BOOK 3

Aftertaste

Book 4

Chapter 1

My emotions really don't seem to know what to do with themselves. My belly aches with the emptiness that comes from Professor Charlton's apparent rejection. At the same time, my heart swells and races at the little thread of hope she dangled before me just as I left.

Really, that sums up the nature of our relationship—if *relationship* is even what it can be called. She whips me into a frenzy and then casts me aside. She lets me get a taste of her, both literally and metaphorically, and then shuts down.

I crave her now. She's like some blend of junk food and drugs for my soul. Which, when I put it in those words, makes this whole dealio seem beyond simply unhealthy. Maybe there's utter devastation on the horizon. For our relationship, but more tellingly, for me. My heart, soul and pussy.

As I pull up outside my apartment building, the heat of my desire for the prof still pulses through me. It never seems to fade, no matter how much I try to push it down. I swear she's left a mark deep in my mind. Burned her brand into my very soul.

And now I'm so fucking scared of what that means. Throughout our brief and torrid time together, all she's ever given me is hot and cold. The cold times sting like frostbite, but I'll take those every time, because the heat is otherworldly.

What scares me most of all is the thought that she'll come to her senses, and that it could be any day now. She'll realize I'm not what she truly needs. I'm too raw, too innocent, too lame.

Maybe I'm just some weird little fuck she can use to scratch an itch. Maybe in the end she needs something or someone

I'm not. Someone less clingy. Fuck, maybe someone less female. She was married to a man before, for fuck's sake. For all I know, I'm just the highest unchecked item on her bucket list, and she's about to draw a line through me.

And yet, she still keeps me coming back. I'm not even sure why I love it.

Except maybe, just maybe... I love *her*.

Oh, fuck. That word again. Another thing I can't seem to push down. It's as if she's cast a spell on me, and she's the only one who could ever break it. I can't escape the feeling, and I don't even want to.

I need her to need me.

So, I'll do what she tells me. Go where she says. Wear whatever she asks.

And I'll absolutely be there tomorrow. Ready, wet and willing.

Chapter 2

I'M PRETTY CLUELESS ABOUT fashion, but I know a few basic terms, so I had a little bit of direction when I hit the thrift store yet again this afternoon. They're gonna know me by name soon enough.

I hit a chintzy goldmine when I found the bridesmaids' dress selection. Luckily, there was a single tasteful option there. An A-line floor length number with a plunging V-neck. Soft pink, almost as pale as my skin, and—for once—exactly my size. The hip-high slit is just a bonus. It's a tough dress to drive in, but it's worth it.

To my surprise, Professor Charlton is waiting outside the destination for me when I arrive. Her face lights up for the briefest of instants when she looks me up and down. A lightning strike of passion that burns itself into my retinas.

This dress is *so* worth it.

"Come, cherie," she says, holding out her hand. Tonight, she's dressed almost like she would for classes, but with pants instead of a skirt. Minimal makeup, with her hair apparently tucked down into the back of her wide-shouldered blazer.

In fact, despite her beauty and the curvy, wide-hipped shape of her luscious body, she's presenting an almost masculine front. She even has a tie on.

The location she's brought me to is a classy but sedate free-standing building, in a part of town I've never even come close to. If I had to guess, I'd say this place is a high-end club of some kind.

She leads me inside, past the wall of immense but unremarkable security dudes. The interior is dimly lit and cozy, with dozens of tables covered with charcoal gray tablecloths. Each table has a little sign that says *RESERVED*, and something that looks like a vintage wooden ping-pong racket. Soft jazz plays through the sound system, and that somehow puts me more at ease.

A gorgeous, dark-skinned woman apparently materializes from the shadows and walks over to us, then leads us to a table. It's in the back corner of the room, in almost complete darkness.

Professor Charlton pulls out a chair for me, like a gentleman would. I'll have my back to the rest of the room if I sit there, and that makes me fucking uneasy. But how can I refuse?

"Please, my little pudding," she says, gesturing toward the seat, and I slide my ass down onto it.

The prof eases into the chair across from me, and for a long time, she just stares at me. It's like she's studying me, but I don't know what she's looking for. Whatever it is, I hope she finds it.

I have no doubt this is another of her wild little games. And in truth, it shouldn't surprise me. By coming tonight, I've essentially signed up to be a little mouse for this sexy kitty to play with. And so long as I get a taste of *her* sexy kitty, I'll do whatever she needs.

Still, my silly, impulsive nature bubbles through me, as if my blood is champagne. I need to know what the fuck is going on here, but I don't want to be the one to break first. Let her tell me, rather than me begging to know.

That desperation gets the better of me, but rather than blurt out the questions running through my whirlwind mind, I fall back on old habits and bring my fingers across so I can pinch my wrist. Professor Charlton bursts into action, grasping my hand before I can make contact.

Her grip on me is firm and commanding, and it sends a shiver through me that ends up straight in my pussy. She releases me and I press both my palms to the table.

"Good girl," she murmurs. It's little more than a hum, but those are the words that always—*always*—make me soft in all the best places.

She leans back in her chair and signals off to the side, her eyes never leaving mine. I'm not sure if she's weighing me up or wearing me down. All I do know is she's teasing the living fuck out of me, and she knows it. It's there in the sexy, evil glint in her dark, soulful eyes. It's there in the cunning upward arc at the corner of her perfect, kissable lips.

A waiter seems to materialize beside us, like the hostess did earlier. Professor Charlton orders a whiskey for herself and an orange juice for me. Is she playing it safe because I'm only 19? Or is there some other—maybe darker—reason she's keeping the alcohol away from me.

Our drinks arrive, and I frown when I see mine has a fucking umbrella in it, and a goddamn silly straw. Like I'm a child. Is this another of the prof's jokes? One more test to see how I react? Sure, I call her mama and she calls me her sweet baby, but since that only happens when we're fucking, then surely it's just a kinky role play. Right?

"Drink up, my little pudding. Show time is nearly here."

"Show time?"

The prof takes a hearty slug of her drink and then points over my shoulder with the same hand that's holding her tumbler. I turn to look and I just about jump in surprise. The entire place is now filled with people. All of them sitting at their tables, and all facing the same way. Away from me.

That's when I notice there's a set of ornate curtains across the entire wall that's far behind me. The kind they use in theaters.

And suddenly, it dawns on me. This is a private club, and whatever is about to happen is going to happen right here, right now, in front of all these strangers.

Professor Charlton finishes her drink and gets to her feet. "Come, cherie. It's time."

Chapter 3

SHE TAKES ME BY the elbow and leads me through a small door to the side of the stage. Once we're inside, she turns me toward a large mirror and fusses with my hair. She fluffs it out so it cascades down over my shoulders, and then she smooths it down.

It's like she's preparing me for the stage. Oh god. She is, isn't she? *I'm* the show.

When she's done, she turns me back to face her and gives me a once-over. "Delightful."

"What's, um...going on?" A few minutes ago, I gnashed and wailed inside my head about being treated like a child. Now I sound just like one.

"It's auction night, my little pudding."

My expression must have asked all the questions for me. Professor Charlton kisses my forehead, then wipes at the spot, even though she's barely wearing any lipstick. "A trust exercise, Giselle."

"Oh, okay. I'm gonna have to jump off the edge of the stage and you'll all catch me, right?"

The prof bites her lovely bottom lip as she smiles. "You are just too adorable, cherie. No, nothing like that."

"Then—"

"Shh." She presses her finger to my lips, and even though she's tormenting me, I have to fight the urge to flick my tongue out. Draw that slender digit into my mouth. Suck on it as if it's her nipple. Her clit. "After your magnificent showing last night, many of my colleagues expressed an interest in...getting to know you better."

"Uh..."

"Several of those men out there are multi-millionaires, cherie. You could do much worse."

"Men?" I mean, I haven't really put a label on myself or anything, but I can't imagine ever wanting a man the way I want Professor Charlton. I don't even think it's a gender thing anymore. It's just *her*. "Wait..."

"Oh, yes. You've never been with a man, though. Have you, cherie?"

I clamp my mouth shut and glare at the floor as I shake my head no. I guess technically I'm still a virgin. At least by last century's standards. But that's not something I plan to do anything about at all, and especially not with some random dude. Rich as fuck, or poor as dirt, I'm just not interested while ever Professor Charlton has me on her invisible leash.

When I grow brave enough to look back up at the prof, I realize she's studying me again. This time, like I'm a textbook. A few more seconds pass before she softens and smiles, and then boops my nose with her finger.

"So pale," she says, little more than a hum. "Let's see if I can put some color in those soft cheeks."

Professor Charlton leans in and takes my lips in a soft kiss, and I open my mouth instantly. Automatically. She delves her sweet tongue inside me and I grip her shoulders, fisting the sleeves of her masculine blazer.

I sense movement down lower and it takes me a moment to realize she's slid her hand into the side slit of my fancy dress. She's pulling it aside to reveal my damp underwear.

For a moment, the skin of my legs soaks up the cool air. Then the prof presses her hand to the front of my panties and that's the only thing I can feel in the entire world. Her fingers on my clit. Even through the thin fabric of my underwear, it's still so rich and intense I want to cry out.

Then she thrusts her fingers down past the elastic waist-band and strokes downward and into the slick heart of my cunt. She pumps her hand up and down, forward and back, still thrusting her tongue in and out of my mouth.

I hook one hand around the back of her neck and cry out, and she absorbs the wailing sound with her mouth. She swallows my voice as she takes me right up to the crest of my orgasm, and then she pinches my clit so hard I just about black out.

My entire body vibrates with a shuddering climax, and I'm certain I've left scratch marks on Professor Charlton's neck. She seems not to have even noticed. Just keeps grinding her fingers over my clit, harder and harder, until my orgasm finally eases.

The prof breaks our kiss and slips her fingers out of my panties. She locks eyes with me and then thrusts those glistening fingers straight into her mouth, humming with pure pleasure as she drinks down my taste. Then she pulls them out with a wet popping sound and glides them into my mouth.

"You are nectar, my little pudding," she murmurs, and I suckle on her skin, drowning in her beautiful dark eyes as I float on the rich taste of my arousal.

When she takes her fingers out again, she kisses me and steps back. She presses her palms to my cheeks and smiles. "There's the lovely pink we need. We're selling the sizzle, not the steak."

"Fuck," I whisper. "What are you doing to me?" I don't mean just now, either. I mean every single thing she's done, and everything she's planning. What the hell is going on?

As always, Professor Charlton seems to get me, without me explaining myself. "Do not fret, my little pudding. Those people out there are unaware of it, but this is nothing more than a game. A cock-tease. You walk on stage, strut your lovely stuff, and they bid on you."

"And what do they get if they win?"

"Well, you, sweet baby. And you take 80% of the winning bid. The house takes the rest."

"No, but...what do they *get?* From me?"

"Ah. The winner takes you away and does whatever they want with your perfect little derriere."

"Hey! I didn't agree to—"

She holds her hand up again, and I'm silenced. "Cherie. Did I not assure you already that this is a trust exercise? *Trust* me. As high as anyone else goes, I will outbid them." She draws me into an embrace that feels loving. To me, at least. "Does it not excite you to be valued so highly, even by strangers?"

I swallow in nervousness and then nod. There's no doubt I should feel some kind of negativity about it all. Contempt? Revulsion, even? But the truth is, Professor Charlton has just stripped away one more layer of my emotional onion. I've lived a life without a whole lot of approval from the people who matter, right up until this woman took me under her wing and into her bed. Well, against her desk.

So, to learn that there are dozens of other people—strangers or not—who find me somehow worthy, honestly, *does* make a difference. We all want to be wanted, after all.

Professor Charlton slides her hands down my body and caresses my ass. "Did you really think I would let anyone else get their hands on your sweet body, my little pudding?"

I truly don't know which way's even up at the moment, so I sink my head against the bed of her breasts, warm even through the shirt, tie and blazer she's wearing, and I put my arms around her waist.

"Huh," I say, feeling something different. "Your belt buckle's digging into my belly."

"Hm," she says, and I can't tell if it's a grunt or a laugh. Far too soon, the prof eases me out of her embrace, and takes a gentle hold of my shoulders.

"It's time, cherie."

Chapter 4

Before I can say a word, she walks up the stairs and onto the stage. I'm alone with my reflection, and it's clear that once again, I'm about to be on display for a bunch of strangers.

But fuck it. I'll do whatever the professor asks. Just to please her. And if it makes me a slut, well...so be it. I'm *her* slut.

Professor Charlton comes back to the top of the stairs and calls me to join her, and then she leads me out onto the stage.

"This is your mark, cherie. Remember, I will be out there, bidding on you. It's a game. It's a tease. And it's all about trust." She gives me a quick peck on the lips. "Do you trust me, my sweet baby?"

"I trust you, mama."

She closes her eyes, and I swear it's an expression of bliss that crosses her beautiful face. And then she's gone.

A minute later, the curtains part, and there's a low murmur of appreciation from the audience. I'm certain my pussy has been struck by a lightning bolt.

"My, my, my," a sultry baritone voice says through the sound system. "What a magnificent item we have up for auction tonight."

I swallow and strive to keep my expression neutral. For some reason, being objectified still feels better than being overlooked. At least they *see* me.

"Please give a warm welcome to the lovely Miss Giselle."

I'm not sure what I expected, but this is nothing like the crowd at a sporting event or a regular theater. There's no raucous applause or hooting. No whistling. The entire audience is in darkness and I'm lit up like a fucking Christmas tree, so I can't see anyone. But it sounds like they're gently knocking the tops of their tables with those wooden rackets.

"Tonight, Miss Belmont is our only item up for auction. She's a first year college student, standing five feet, five inches tall, with a delightfully firm and feminine young body. As you can all see, she is an exquisite natural beauty."

I can't believe how good it feels to hear those words, even from a stranger. From a *man*. It's like I'm a work of art, or a rare jewel. Like I'm valuable.

"And as a bonus," the voice continues, "Miss Giselle is an increasingly rare commodity in this day and age, as she is yet to know the touch of a man."

My breath freezes instantaneously. How the fuck is that the business of these people? And how the fuck did Professor Charlton think it was fine to tell everyone I'm a fucking virgin?

"As such, she is, naturally, a premium item. Let us start the bidding at $1,000."

My heart stops in my chest. No way he just said that. A cool grand? For a skittish little lame-ass like me?

By now I can just barely make out the low lit audience, and someone down there raises their wooden paddle thing. I see there's a number on it.

"Excellent," the voice says. "Do I hear $2,000?"

They're going up by thousands?

"$2,000 to you, sir. Any advance?"

I struggle to breathe as the bids climb into what feels to me like the stratosphere. Within two minutes we've passed $10,000 and I worry I'm gonna wet myself from the pressure of it all. How the fuck will I live up to that kind of money? I've never even seen a proper cock in the flesh, let alone touched one. Am I going to have to put it in my mouth? Between my legs? Fuck, for that kind of money, they're gonna make me take it in the ass, aren't they?

Then I remember Professor Charlton's promise. That she'll outbid everyone. That she'll take me home and have her fucking way with me. Believing that helps me to relax. I know now she's the only person—woman or man—who I'd ever let take me in the ass.

The bidding continues to climb, and I'm honestly not sure how much money is going back and forth here. This is, like, a year's tuition. Maybe my entire course. It's all a blur to me as I strive just to stand still. Keep my back straight and my legs from melting.

After a few minutes, the voice announces that we've reached the final call for bids, and then it's just a matter of waiting for the paddles to go up. It's like watching a tennis match, only in slow motion. And with more rackets.

This is a whole other world to anything I've ever known. A world that's more money than sense. I lose track of the bidding, but the voice announces that I'm sold at $75,000.

"Congratulations, Mr Matthews."

Wait...what? Mister Matthews? *Mister?*

Chapter 5

I'M JUST ABOUT HYPERVENTILATING as I try to process this. Professor Charlton said...she promised. The house lights come up a little and I whip my head around, glaring up at the corner where we sat before. And of course, she's not there.

She's fucked me. I know it's meant to be a game, but games have rules. And she's just broken the biggest one.

The woman who greeted us at the beginning comes in from the side of the stage.

"Please, come this way," she says, leading me off to the side. I put up no resistance. All the fight has gone from my body. I'm more alone in the world right now than I ever was before. Because I let myself believe in someone. Believe I mattered to them.

The dark-skinned beauty leads me into a small office and hands me an envelope full of cash. "There you go, Miss Belmont. $60,000. The house keeps the other 15."

The envelope is so much lighter than I would've thought, and yet I can barely hold it up. It's just a wad of paper that means nothing to me. At least back at home, I was always worthless. I had nowhere to fall when mom cut me down.

Professor Charlton made me soar into the sky, and this fall is going to hurt for fucking years.

I push the envelope back at the hostess. "No, I can't. I'm not going through with—"

She refuses to take it. "Keep the money, Miss Belmont. It's yours. We have a strict policy of no refunds."

"That's not what I—"

She takes me by the elbow and leads me out the back door. It's a little like being in the theater, except there's a parking lot and a dumpster out back.

"Miss Belmont, your ride is here." She nods toward a sleek black Rolls-Royce. A man in a tux stands beside it, holding the door open.

"Is that...?"

"That's Mr Matthews, yes."

So that's it. Professor Charlton has pimped me off to one of her buddies. A man, no less. Just fucking dandy. And if that's how it's gonna be, then fuck it. I might as well milk it for all it's worth. Screw the prof. She had me and she's tossed me away.

"Fine," I blurt. "I guess it's about time I finally got myself some cock." Not that I want it. I'm still not sure if I have a label I want to stick onto myself, but I know neither straight nor even bi-curious is a fit for me.

I march over to the car, trying to plaster a smile on my face for the presumably nice man who's thrown out 75 grand on a chick with no game, and who'll have to keep her eyes closed all the way through. Who'll probably burst into an ugly cry the instant he whips his dick out.

"Welcome, Giselle," he says, drawing the door open even wider.

I hold my breath and steel myself as I slide into the back of the fancy-pants car. Even the luxury leather on the seats feels cold to me, though. How the fuck have I come to this? I'm just a toy for all these rich fucks to play with. Not even a pawn, since chess at least has some class about it. I'm not even a fucking checker. I'm nothing more than a plastic fucking marble for one of these hungry hippos to devour.

Mr Matthews climbs into the driver's seat and starts the engine. It's pure, understated luxury and yet it might as well be a fucking nondescript white van. He says nothing to me. Just drives out of the alley and out onto the streets, taking me to my fate.

He pulls into the underground garage of a crazy-expensive hotel. I'm still numb as he opens my door and helps me out. His touch is gentle, but because of what's coming, it feels almost like a violation. Thankfully, he doesn't talk to me, doesn't crowd me...doesn't even try to touch my hand as we ride the elevator to the presidential suite. The guy's clearly fucking loaded, but even as poor as I am, I don't give the slightest flying fuck.

The cold, sucking pit of emotion inside me is just like the one I used to feel when I was a kid. When mom would assume every broken toy, every spilled drink, every mess of any kind must have been my fault. How my little sister Jeanette would either blame me for shit she did, or just stay silent while mom ranted at me.

In short, I'm fucking triggered, and it hurts so much more right now than ever. At least with mom, I can't remember a single time she truly supported me in any way. She was cold, she was nasty, but she was at least consistent as fuck.

The problem is, Professor Charlton has lifted me from that swamp. Held me up with her fucking angel wings, as far as I'm concerned. She's flown me too close to the sun, so that now I've fallen, the impact hurts like hell.

What I've had with her has been sweet as anything. But now, I'm left with nothing but a bitter aftertaste.

The elevator doors open onto the massive suite itself. Even from here, the view of the city is mind-numbing. This is a realm of existence I've only ever seen in movies.

Mr Matthews steps forward and holds out his hand to me. "Please, Giselle?"

A deal's a deal, I guess. I walk out of the elevator, but can't seem to stop staring at the floor. I watch my hand moving as if it's completely independent, as I reach across to grip my wrist and give it the pinching from fucking hell.

"No, cherie."

Chapter 6

I JUMP LIKE I'VE just heard a rattlesnake hissing, even taking a halting step backward. There, on the sofa, sits Professor Charlton.

"W–what...?"

"Welcome, my little pudding," she says, then turns toward Mr Matthews. "Thank you, Richard."

"Of course, Alicia. Goodnight."

Then he turns, marches back into the elevator, and ceases to exist for me.

"What the fuck?" My voice is squeaky with anger and confusion. "You didn't even...even bid for me!"

"Sweet baby," she says. "That was the game. The trust exercise. I had Richard bidding on my behalf."

I hold still, glaring at this woman—my dream lover who seems determined to cut me to pieces—and my wrist positively itches with the need to be pinched.

"Giselle," the prof continues. "You know how I feel about you. Don't you?"

I squeeze my mouth tighter shut, like a toddler whose only escape from punishment would be a lie. Who knows from bitter experience that a lie discovered will bring even greater punishment.

In truth, I have no idea how she feels about me. Not really. She likes to tease me, apparently loves to make me come, over and over again. But that's all about *her* wants and desires.

"My little pudding," the prof says. "You said you trusted me."

"I did." I shake my head. "But you promised me something pretty concrete and delivered something else."

"Cherie—"

"I'm tired of always feeling lost. Feeling like the stupidest person in the room. Like some fucking trailer trash piece of ass that everyone looks down on."

There's silence for a moment and then Professor Charlton stands slowly and comes toward me, like she's approaching a trapped little lamb. I'm numb now. A statue. I put up no fight as she pulls me to her body and holds me tighter than she ever has.

As hard as I want to hate her, I simply can't. Not when I'm wrapped up in the blanket of her body, breathing in the sweet scents of her skin and her hair. I go loose as she brings me across to the couch and sits me down on it.

Professor Charlton kneels before me and slides my heels off, one at a time. She caresses each foot gently, then works her hands higher up my legs. I'm still numb and I haven't yet thawed to her completely, but despite that, I can't keep my breathing under control.

To my surprise, she keeps her hands outside my dress and away from my pussy and my tits. She leans forward and puts her soft palms on either side of my neck. I fall into the majesty of her dark eyes yet again as she studies me. Yet again.

"I wholeheartedly apologize for misjudging tonight, cherie. It was never my intention to hurt you, or make you feel less than the magnificent creature you are. The truth is..." She swallows, and when she continues, there's a liquid quality in her voice that sounds for all the world like vulnerability. "Well, you must realize you are not the first woman I've brought into my world in this way."

I shut my eyes and nod. At this point, it seems clear that from day one, I've just been her latest little fuck toy. Professor Charlton cups my chin in her hand and waits until I open my eyes again.

"But a more potent truth is that I've never done this with one of my students before. Rules being what they are, and all. With you, I find myself…" She pauses and swallows. "The truth is, you have become my world."

She kisses me, then, and it's somehow different, somehow deeper than any kiss we've shared before. It's soft, and it's sweet. It's like coming home. And when we part, she wipes at my cheeks and the tears I didn't even realize had fallen.

"I want to rail against those who've brought you down, my gorgeous girl. The ones who've made you doubt your own magic. Tonight was supposed to let you see how truly glorious you are." She frowns and shakes her head, as if confused. "And yet, I misjudged the tone, in a way I never have before. Tonight, I became that which I despise. I, too, brought you down."

Chapter 7

I TAKE HOLD OF her wrists and squeeze them, like I usually squeeze my own. There are dozens of questions rolling around inside my head, and I can't capture any single one long enough to ask it.

"The absolute truth is, I'm afraid of losing you now, Giselle. And I know there's so much you've not yet experienced. Things maybe you believe I can't give you."

"Like what?"

"Like a thick, hard cock." She smiles, and there's a mischievous sparkle in her eyes. "That's why I asked Richard to bid on my behalf. I needed to see how you'd react to the idea of being with a man."

I shake my head, and it's a mix of denial and relief. Before I can find my words, she kisses me and stands, removing her wide-shouldered blazer. I watch, rapt, as she removes her tie and unbuttons her dress shirt.

When she's down to just a bra on top, she shakes her head and her lush, feminine mane flies out around her like a halo, then settles gently on her shoulders.

"Do you wonder, cherie? What it's like to be with a man?"

She's been painfully honest with me since I got here. I figure I owe her the same.

"I...guess I'm curious. But I'm with *you*, aren't I?" The words might sound like a challenge. Like I'm trying some passive-aggressive misdirection to avoid speaking the truth. But I'm just desperate for clarification. That we're a couple of some description.

"Curiosity is natural, my sweet baby. I encourage it, of course." She slips off her bra and reaches for her dress pants, and I notice she's not actually wearing a belt. So what was it that was poking me in the belly before?

When she drops the pants, that question is answered. And several more come barging into my head. Instead of sexy panties, or even going commando, Professor Charlton is wearing a strap-on dildo.

"Perhaps I can help you explore your...curiosity."

"Ohhh..." I can't stop staring at the sex toy. It's cool blue and shiny, standing proud from the black harness around the professor's hips and thighs. Every move she makes, no matter how small, gets the toy dancing, and I can't help but follow the movements. It's not a huge one—thank fuck—but it's still bigger than anything I've ever had inside me.

I reach out slowly, like it's an angry snake. Like I can charm it with the smooth movements of my hand.

"Yes, cherie. Touch me. Touch my big, hard cock."

Oh, Christ. I know it's a game, or maybe more of a role play. But her words ignite me from the inside, and I can't believe just how much I want this thing inside me. And all because it's attached to this incredible woman.

The dildo is warm to the touch, from being pressed against her magnificent body in those pants. I grip it with only my fingers, almost like the clumsy way I held a cigarette, the one and only time I tried smoking back in high school. Professor Charlton gasps as I move my hand forward and back, as if the toy literally radiates pleasure to her.

"Please, my little pudding," she moans. "Put it in your mouth."

"Oh, god…"

I lick my lips and scoot my ass forward on the couch. Professor Charlton rests one hand on the top of my head and guides me forward, and I open my mouth. I pause at the tip of the toy and flick it with my tongue, and even that seems to give her some kind of thrill. She lets out a tiny moan and bumps her hips gently forward, driving the rounded tip between my lips.

"That's it, my sweet baby. Take me all the way in."

Jesus. I've obviously never given head, but just as obviously, I know the basics of what's involved. But as she drives her plastic cock deeper and deeper inside me, and I catch traces of her musky sweet arousal, she makes me believe I can fucking do anything.

I open my mouth wide and let the prof pump her toy inside, and then she moves her hand to the back of my neck. She fucks my mouth, slowly and gently at first. And then faster and harder as she gets going. I slide forward, landing on my knees before this magnificent woman. Now I'm really getting into my role, and I move my hands out to her hips as I caress the dildo with my tongue and lips. I can't believe how good it feels to have this in my mouth. How much it turns me on.

But there's no way I can take the entire toy into my throat. I'm not that experienced. I pull back with a gagging sound that makes me feel silly all over again.

"Oh, my. You are wonderful, cherie," the prof whispers. "Strip for me, please?"

Chapter 8

THERE'S NO HESITATION NOW. I simply slide the shoulder straps down my arms and push the dress to the floor. Never once breaking eye contact with the powerful woman standing over me. I practically fling my bra across the room and stand only long enough to kick my soaked panties off.

Professor Charlton's eyes soften as she gazes over my bare body. "So fucking beautiful," she moans, and it reminds me what a rarity it is to hear curse words spilling from her luscious mouth.

She narrows those lovely eyes a moment later and pushes me back down onto the couch, following along with me. She comes down onto her knees between my legs and takes my throat in her hand. Not squeezing so much as just holding. She rolls her fingers and thumb, then strokes that hand down between my breasts. Her touch is warm and gentle, and it makes me feel like the most precious thing in the world.

When she reaches my pussy, she's so tender I just about melt. She slides her fingers down either side of my slit, and then she seems to abandon any form of self control.

Professor Charlton makes a fierce snarling sound as she drops between my thighs and plants her gorgeous mouth over my pussy. She moans with pleasure as she strokes her incredible tongue up and down, and I pull my legs up to let her come closer. Go deeper.

She takes hold of one of my tits and squeezes it all to hell, pinching my nipple between her thumb and her palm as she works that breast like dough.

I grip the back of her head and cry out in pleasure as she whirls her tongue in circles around my clit, and then teases my opening with her fingertips.

"Oh, god. Please fuck me, mama."

She pulls back and gazes at me with undiluted lust in her eyes. Her beautiful face glows, painted as it is with my juices. Then she grasps my hips and slides my ass closer.

The tip of her toy kisses my cunt, and I gasp as my eyes fly wide with anticipation.

"Are you ready, my sweet baby?"

"Yes, mama. Oh, god, I need your enormous cock inside me, mama."

"Jesus fucking Christ," she hisses, and for the first time I can recall, her crisp and cultured accent crumbles away. The words come out like she's a London street thug saying them. Coarse and savage and so fucking hot.

Professor Charlton guides the rounded head of her dildo into my opening and captures me with her eyes.

"Do it, mama. Please?"

"Irresistible fucking strumpet," she growls. "I need to see your beautiful face when I bust your little cherry." Then she thrusts her hips forward. The toy fills me with one brutal pump, and the pain is easily as harsh as the pleasure is sweet. I wail as she stretches me like nobody else ever has.

Or ever will.

She pistons her hips in a steady rhythm, driving faster and deeper with every beautiful drive. Her big tits bounce and sway as she fucks me senseless.

I snake my legs around her waist and squeeze her wide hips in a fucking vice grip. The prof pumps even more fiercely and I'm fuller than I've ever been, and wider open than I'd imagined was possible.

I know now, all I want is to be fucked by this incredible woman. Every which fucking way. I was already a slut for her perfect pussy. Now, I'm a whore for her cock as well.

My entire body is alight with pleasure, and I can hardly breathe. I try to grind my hips up against the strap-on, but I just don't have the experience to know quite how to move.

"Take it all, cherie," she moans. "Take my hard cock deep inside your tight little virgin cunt."

"Mama..." I moan. "Oh, god..."

Professor Charlton barely draws a breath as she pulls her toy out of me and flips me over onto my front. She pulls my ass up and I fall forward on the couch, my knees still on the floor. She shoves her toy back inside me from behind, and I thrust my tight ass back against her.

She pounds me with her play cock, every drive grinding past my clit. I'm practically screaming with pleasure. My pussy is dripping wet and my clit is hard and pulsing.

The prof strokes a finger down the crack of my ass and presses it against my asshole. I cry out as she penetrates me there, and it feels so fucking good.

She pumps her toy in and out of me, and she keeps pulsing that finger in and out of my ass.

"Mama…mama…I'm gonna come."

"Come for me, sweet baby girl. Come for mama."

My taboo lover grips my hair in a tight fist and pulls, and that's the last straw. My skin crackles and my core ignites, and I come like a mountain waterfall, crying and wailing as ecstasy fills me beyond overflowing.

Professor Charlton groans and slams her toy balls-deep inside me, and I can feel her body shuddering. When it's over, she slumps against me, and we both slide onto the floor, spent and sweating and trembling. She kisses me and caresses my back, and whispers soft, soothing words I can't even make out.

She seems to think we're done. She needs to think again.

Chapter 9

I SLIDE MY MOUTH down from hers, kissing her throat and the sweet space between her tits.

"Cherie," she says, her perfect cultured accent back in place. "What are you...?"

I press her big boobs together and bite into one nipple, and then the other. She gasps with pleasure and pain, and I kiss a trail down her soft belly. Her big toy pokes into me, and I grip the sides of the harness. I have no idea how to work the thing so I just haul down on it. It needs to go. I've already had her toy cock. Now I need the real thing.

Her pussy.

"Oh, my little pudding. You know I don't...I can't allow..."
I kiss her glistening mound the instant I bare it, and she

sighs. And when she speaks again, it's that rough, Cockney accent she's been hiding all this time. "Aw, fuck yeah..."

Suddenly, it all clicks into place for me. How she uses control of her lover as a mask for herself. And how she's let it slip further and further, every time we're together.

Maybe this has all been part of the game. Maybe this is even a practical application for the course she's teaching. All I know is, I've found my place in life, and I'm certain she has, too.

"Alicia," I moan. "I'll always be your sweet baby. I know that. I'll submit to Professor Charlton. But I'll give myself over totally to the *real* you...Alicia."

"Bloody hell, sweetheart..." she whispers, gazing into my eyes like she finally understands that I'm a home for her, as much as she is for me.

It takes me only a moment to get the harness down her legs and off. I send it sailing off into the darkness of the room and gaze down into the sweet, glistening heart of Alicia Charlton's gorgeous cunt.

"Sweetheart," she moans, and as much as I loved her upper class tones...hearing the real Alicia is just so much hotter. "Fuck, nobody has ever looked at me like that."

"I see you, Alicia," I say, echoing her words from before. "I see you in a way you seem unwilling or unable to see yourself. I see you like nobody else can, mama."

"Sweet baby."

I shove her thighs wide apart and dive between them, pressing my tongue to her wet opening and dragging it up to her clit. She grasps my hair and cries out, and I take her clit into my mouth, sucking gently at first.

"That's it, Giselle," she moans. "Eat me, my sweet baby. Fuck my pussy with your tongue."

I'm not sure if it's her words or her taste or just her fucking amazing body, but I'm dizzy with lust as I thrust my tongue into her, and then glide back up to her clit.

"Make me come, sweet baby. Oh, god, I want to come all over your beautiful face."

I think maybe I go into a trance. It's like I'm looking down at myself, licking and sucking and nibbling on Alicia's hard clit and soft lips. Watching as I pump my fingers in and stroke the magic bump deep inside her.

And then I come back into myself as I look up and lock eyes with her. I flick my tongue hard and fast across Alicia's clit. She grits her teeth and groans, and then she comes with a powerful shuddering that seems to come from her core.

"Fuck me," she cries, and it's in that gutter accent I heard, ever so briefly, before. Like she's really the daughter of some street vendor. Like she's done everything she can to better herself. Move away from a past that jars against who she believes she truly is. "Fuck me, sweet baby. I need you, Giselle. I...I fucking love you."

I plunge my fingers back into her and lap at her clit, and then I slide down and thrust my tongue inside her. Her salty sweetness bursts into my senses and I swear it melds with my blood. Alicia rocks her hips back and forth, fucking herself against my tongue.

She quivers again, and this time it's a softer, gentler climax, but it lasts so much longer. Finally she lets out a long sigh and goes still, and I keep tonguing her pussy until I'm sure she's finished. That she's had all she can take.

I crawl up to her, and we wrap our arms around each other. We kiss and kiss, and I'm not sure how much time passes before I realize we're both drifting off.

Sometime during the night we wake, and she takes me through to the massive bed, and we make love again and again before fatigue takes us over.

I drift off to sleep with the sweetest aftertaste dancing across my tongue.

When I open my eyes again, it's daylight outside the massive windows, and the sky is a beautiful pink-gold. I'm in bed with my woman. She's as perfect in sleep as she is awake, and I could never get enough of her.

I'll even play all her games, now I understand what trust truly means.

Alicia stirs against me, and I stroke her sweet face with my still fragrant fingers. She comes awake and gazes up into my eyes.

"Giselle," she murmurs, her high class accent back in place. "I'm in a lot of trouble, cherie."

I know we're in a world of mess. We've blown the university's rules out of the water, in no uncertain terms.

"Worth it?" I ask her.

"For me, absolutely." She pauses, and the slightest look of concern crosses her beautiful face. "Is it worth it for you?"

I smile as I shake my head. Like I can't believe she even needs to ask. But I place my head down on her bountiful breasts and sigh out my answer.

"Yes, mama."

END OF THE SERIES

For more Sapphic Sexytimes, check out all my big, wet box sets!

- **LESBIAN AGE GAP EROTICA**
- **LUSTFUL LESBIANS**
- **LUSTFUL LESBIANS BOOK 2**
- **HER FIRST WOMAN**
- **FEMME FANTASIES**
- **QUICK, SLICK & LONGING TO LICK**

About the author

Spicy stories of women loving women. Okay, so there's plenty of red hot lust, too.

Kitty is the sapphic-scribing alter-ego of Steph Brothers.